ABOUT THE AUTHOR

Peter Matthiessen is the author of more than thirty books and the only writer to win the National P̶ ̶ ̶ ̶rd for both non-fiction (*The Snow Le̶*̶ ̶ ̶ies, in 1979 and 1980) and f̶ ̶ ̶8). A co-founder of *The* ̶ ̶ned naturalist, explorer ̶

Praise for *In Paradise*

'Darkly humorous.'   *The Herald*

'There is much to meditate on and many reasons to read this novel.'   *The Times*

'A deeply intelligent study of Holocaust remembrance... Bleakly funny and eloquent.'   *Wall Street Journal*

'A dark but thoroughly testing, ambitious and thought-provoking novel.'   *Curious Animal*

'Like the rest of Matthiessen's vast body of work, *In Paradise* leads us into questions that define our most profound mysteries.'   *Washington Post*

'*In Paradise* allows Peter Matthiessen to once again dem-onstrate that he remains one of our most powerful writers.'
                                        Miami Herald

In Paradise

PETER MATTHIESSEN

ONEWORLD

A Oneworld Book

First published in Great Britain by Oneworld Publications, 2014

This paperback edition published by Oneworld Publications in 2014

Published by arrangement with Riverhead Books, a division of
Penguin Group (USA) LLC, A Penguin Random House Company

ISBN 978-1-78074-608-1
ISBN 978-1-78074-556-5 (eBook)

Printed and bound in Great Britain by Clays Ltd, St Ives plc
Book design by Meighan Cavanaugh

Oneworld Publications
10 Bloomsbury Street
London WC1B 3SR
England

Stay up to date with the latest books,
special offers, and exclusive content from
Oneworld with our monthly newsletter

Sign up on our website
www.oneworld-publications.com

Everything is plundered, betrayed, sold.
Death's great black wing scrapes the air,
Misery gnaws to the bone.
Why then do we not despair?

By day, from the surrounding woods,
cherries blow summer into town;
at night the deep transparent skies
glitter with new galaxies.

And the miraculous comes so close
to the ruined dirty houses—
something not known to anyone at all
But wild in our breast for centuries.

—Anna Akhmatova, 1921

PROLOGUE

He told him this: how as a boy fugitive on a scorched day of wartime, crossing the railroad yards of some defeated city, he is drawn closer by a twitching in the shadow under the last boxcar in a transport shunted off onto a siding. The boxcar is silent. He is barely able to make out the tentacle like a thin tongue that emerges through a crack in the wood floor and inches down in search of something on the rail bed. Withdrawn quickly, it disappears up through a crack, only to reappear a moment later, descending slowly, slowly, then swiftly up and slowly down again and then again, until with a loud BANG of jolted iron, the car jumps forward and the thing falls or is dropped and left behind. And as the transport moves out of the yard, he sees an old belt coiled in a puddle between rails, its buckle glinting in the sunlight like the head of a wet snake.

A GUEST

OF POLAND

ONE

He has flown all night over the ocean from the New World, descending from moon stare and the rigid stars into the murk and tumult of inversion shrouding winter Poland.

From the airport, a cab takes him to the city and sets him down in an empty square where a row of buses, closely parked, face a cracked wall; the cab is gone by the time he discovers they are locked. (The imprisoned air inside, he thinks, must be even colder than this outside weather.) At the corner café he is informed that buses to his destination won't be available before spring, and that he has missed the morning train he would have caught had he been driven to the depot; there will be no other until evening.

At a loss, he drinks black coffee at the counter, scowling at the unshaven traveler reflected in the dirty mirror. His antiquated Polish is eked out by the primitive English of a young couple who have overheard his inquiries about hiring a car and boisterously endorse the waiter's protest that the cost would be far too high. Concerned that a visitor to their fair land has been inconvenienced, they offer to escort him to the small museum he had mentioned: the waiter will keep an eye on his old suitcase. On the way he can admire the Royal Palace and cathedral on Wawel Hill and the St. Mary's Basilica destroyed in the thirteenth century by Asian Tatars and rebuilt in the fourteenth with that strange crowned tower. "Like black icicles!" the girl cries. Thus their guest can at least enjoy the historic center of Poland's oldest city, still so beautiful, they say, because Cracow, like Paris, had been spared bomb and fire in the war. Pardon? Oh no, sir, they giggle, they have never been to Paris!

Exhausted, he trails his merry guides past the medieval Cloth House on the Market Square. Mirek and his lovestruck Wanda will not let him visit this city he knows more about than they do without dragging him into a shop to find a souvenir of Poland. Wanda supervises the selection of a silken lozenge of transparent amber. "For delight your sweetheart in America? Beauty gift for Mama?" This golden drop encasing flecks of ancient insects is the very essence of his native earth, yet its acquisition further sinks his spirits. He knows no one who would have much interest in this scrap of fossil tree sap, never mind "delight." He has no sweetheart, only a married lover he does not much miss—in fact, is rather glad to get a rest from—and no surviving family in the New World. Were they still alive, his father and paternal grandparents would have disapproved this trip, having always warned him against returning to this region of southwest Poland just because he happened to be born there. "You have no memory of that place, and our own memories are sad," his father said.

⚶

THE ONE THING he will make sure he sees in Cracow is the Leonardo da Vinci portrait of a Renaissance girl holding a white winter weasel in her lap. Long ago, his father had shown him a faded reproduction clipped from an art magazine ("She reminds me so of your dear mother!"). Alas, on this cold Sunday of 1996, *Young Woman with Ermine* is locked away behind an obdurate wood door. His guides stare at the notice as if hoping that at any moment it might change its mind. Disappointed for their guest and sensing his annoyance, the poor things are looking a bit desperate.

On the return, in an effort to intrigue them, he relates how over the centuries this portrait of Cecilia Gallerani, Count Ludovico Sforza's adolescent mistress, had wandered in times of war and conquest—sealed up in castle cellars, stolen, sold, and finally recovered, only to be confiscated by Hans Frank, now Governor General of Occupied Poland, and displayed in his office in the Royal Palace—

"Is up there!" Eager to contribute, the girl is pointing at the fortress castle looming in the mist on its rock hill over the river. "We can visit!" shouts Mirek, eager, too.

Inside, they are shown the empty office where the Leonardo—and perhaps also a Raphael, never recovered—might have illumined these drab walls, doubtless vaunted as trophies, spoils of war, by *Hausfrau* Brigitte Frank, she who styled herself "a Queen of Poland" as fit title for so grand a personage as the new lady of the Royal Palace. And perhaps it was this Nazi queen (said to have been detested by her husband) who had seen to the theft of "the Cecilia" in early 1945, when this awful family fled the Red Army rumbling across Poland from the east and installed her in their chalet in Bavaria, from where, eventually, she would be rescued by Allied soldiers rumbling across Poland from the west.

"I have always been a student of that period," he explains, embarrassed by their awe of so much knowledge. But as they make their way outside again into the city, he tells his rapt young friends that rather wonderfully, the masterpiece—one of but four known Leonardo portraits of women, including the *Mona Lisa* and *La Belle Ferronnière*, both in the Louvre—turned up in Paris and was eventually

A GUEST OF POLAND

restored, thank God, to Cracow. "Thanks God!" the lovers agree fervently, at the same time confessing prior ignorance of its existence and also their amazement that a treasure so renowned might ever have been found anywhere in their battered land.

THEY HEAD FOR the warmth of that café in Kasimierz, the old Jewish quarter named after King Kasimierz of the sixteenth century—a "Golden Age," he mentions, of benevolence toward Jews, who were fleeing to Poland from pogroms and persecutions all over Europe. However, his companions, though they nod and smile, cannot come up with any comment on all his information, which he'd hoped might stoke a faltering conversation. He tries to mend his pedantic tone but soon falls back on his research for want of a better antidote to their blithe ignorance, instructing them that in former times, their city was a cultural center of this country's Jewish population. After September 1939, when southwest Poland was seized by the Third Reich, the Jews were driven from their houses into a ghetto over near the river, permitting Obergruppenführer Frank to boast that Cracow was the first *Judenfrei* city in the Occupied Territory.

The girl looks at her companion. *Judenfrei? What can he be telling us?*

"But of course you know your own history much better than some foreigner who has never been here."

"Not even to Cracow?" the girl entreats him, hand circling to summon up its fabled spell. "But you are speak okay Polish," Mirek says, urging their guest to tell them more about this "*Judenfrei*": how amusing that in all their lives they have never met a single Jew, not one!

He watches them chortle at the idea of knowing Jews. "I suppose that's not so strange, under the circumstances," he says. "Very few survived the war and scarcely any have returned even today. Small wonder."

"Is small wonder!" Mirek agrees fervently. "Is small wonder!" the girl says. Uneasy, the lovers peer about them for some trace of missing Jews as if these buildings dark with centuries of soot were rife with Hebrew secrets.

⁂

IN COAL FOG and December rain, the thousand-year-old city lies steeped in his own weariness and melancholy. He has no wish to visit the Old Synagogue, built in the Renaissance. Thank you, he says, but he is too tired from his night of travel. "Okay, no problem," Mirek laughs. "Tired is natural." And Wanda smiles, "Okay, tired is natural, no problem exactly." The lovers hug in celebration of their juicy life (and perhaps also to warm themselves: Mirek wears only a thin white turtleneck under his light leather-type jacket and Wanda a denim jacket with overbold white stitching and an orange faux-fox collar).

So delighted are these lovers with their rare opportunity to practice English that they offer to drive their captive stranger all the way to his destination "just for the fun." Don't be silly, he protests, it is much too far, they will have to return on icy roads in the winter dark— "No, no, sir, please, sir, you are the guest of Poland!" If he insists, the guest of Poland can help pay the petrol, is okay? "Yes, it is okay exactly," the girl laughs. Anyway, her parents live in a nearby town and maybe her boyfriend can stay over, too, if Papa will permit.

꩜

AT THE CAFÉ he retrieves his suitcase while Mirek goes off to fetch the car and Wanda runs to the shop next door and buys him a souvenir postcard of *Young Woman with Ermine*. On her return, to her squeaked delight, he pulls out her chair and seats her, ordering hot cocoa and sweet biscuits, whereupon she presents the postcard: "Your Cecilia, sir! Is more pretty than what I am?" Wanda is attractive in her gamine way and has sensed that the visitor may think so. She flirts gaily, intrigued by his Old World manners, he suspects, and his decent clothes. But being un-sophisticated, she becomes alarmed when, to amuse him-self, he captures her gaze and challenges her coquetry by leaning forward to appraise her face while holding up the postcard for comparison. For sure, she cries, as her eyes seek escape, for sure the gentleman will come visit his Cecilia on his way back through Cracow? She fishes in her red shiny purse for nothing whatsoever while he sits back to summon the waiter (at one time a resident of Queens, New York, and in consequence an authority on the U.S.A.) and orders "Mademoiselle" another chocolate to replace the one which in her nervousness she has mostly spilled onto the round marble top of their café table.

"They say Cracow have more synagogue than Jew," Mirek laughs, returning. The joke is far too knowing from the mouth of a young man born long after the war: surely he has overheard it, picked it up, a worn coin off the side-walk. Turning up his nose at the boy's joke as he sets down Wanda's chocolate, the waiter says that most of this city's old wood synagogues had burned down, and the world-famous Old Synagogue of the Renaissance is mainly visited by tour groups from Israel and the United States.

"Tours group exactly!" Relieved that Mirek has re-turned, the girl burbles happily that this old quarter has really come to life as a tourist attraction, with lively "Jew music" in the Klesmer-Hois and the Ariel café. Doubtless, the stranger says, the few Jews who returned after the war enjoy "Jew music." Though his tone is mild, its edge brings a small wrinkle to that alabaster brow. *Could their guest be a bit sensitive about those Jews?*

"It's all right, miss, I'm not Jewish," he smiles. With his wheaten hair and pale blue eyes and broad high cheekbones, he looks more Slav than they do. "How can she know," hoots Mirek, "if she never seen one?"

Scraping chairs back, all three laugh a bit too long. Over their protests, the stranger pays the bill and tips the waiter. With his father's unwieldy leather suitcase (making its first return journey to the old country) he is stuffed into the back of Mirek's little auto, sitting sideways, knees up to his chin. "Have a nice day, mister," the waiter calls, smirking for some reason. "A nice Polish day."

TWO

The road follows the Vistula upriver westward across the frozen landscape; blue-gray hills of the Tatra Mountains and Slovakia rise in the south. Here and there along the way stand stone houses with steep roofs to shed the snows, most of them guarded by spiked iron fences (wolves and brigands?). These dwellings crowd the road in seeming dread of those dark ranks of evergreens that march down the white faces of the hills beyond like Prussian regiments (or Austro-Hungarian or Russian) crossing some hinterland of Bloody Poland, which has no natural boundaries against invaders.

Toward twilight, the tires *thud-thud-thud* across old rails embedded in the asphalt; traversing the road, the railway disappears into the forest. Presumably those tracks were already in use before the war when Oswiecim, just north-east of the frontier, was a hub for seasonal harvest labor transported across northern Europe—one reason, he supposes, for the town's selection as a terminus. Closing his eyes, he imagines he can feel the vibrations of slow trains that might have jolted across flat country for a fortnight, even hear the creak and shriek of iron couplings; he wonders what was passing through the minds of those train engineers of a half century ago, peering down night corridors of forest—rough soot-faced men, as he envisions them, gnawing black crusts.

Beyond the river bridge, at dusk, roadside sheds draw close to the hunched dwellings; soon all congeal as a provincial town. Leaning forward to be heard over the auto's clatter, he asks Mirek and Wanda if they knew that prewar Oswiecim had been a mostly Jewish community renowned for its hospitality: its name, he has read, may derive from a Yiddish word meaning "guests."

"Yittish." Tasting the word, the girl gazes about her, lips parted. "Near this Oshpitzin I am borned." He cannot resist saying, "I was too," and divulging his surname when they press him. "That is a name well-known in these parts," says Mirek, sensing his passenger's reluctance. Distracting Wanda, he says nobody warned him that his girlfriend was a "Yittish." She tickles his ribs as he twists away in raucous protest, swerving the car with one hand off the wheel. "*Not* a Yittish!" she cries. "Borned in old Yittish *house!*"

He is rattled by their noise and dangerous horseplay. But these kids have been generous and he curbs his agitation, subduing their racket by inquiring about Mirek's life ambitions. It seems the boy had originally intended to study for the priesthood at the Cracow seminary where His Holiness—"first Poland Holiness!" the girl assures him—had trained secretly during the war. But these days . . . Mirek hesitates: his parents no longer seem so set on that commitment.

Wanda grins, stroking Mirek's brush-cropped hair. "Know what his Papa say? He say, 'Better maybe that foolish Wanda than some dirty priest!'" Mirek looks unhappy. "Papa is always jokes," he says.

NIGHT IS FALLING, the main street is almost dark. A dimlit sign reading HOTEL GLOB is watery in the cold rain. Could this dreary-looking hostelry have been the hospitable inn of Old Oshpitzin? (It suits his mood to pretend that its glottal name does not signify "World Hotel" but instead commemorates some bloody-minded "Glob the Ogre" of medieval folktales.)

When Mirek halts to ask directions, a townsman sidles up to the car window and peers in, hand brimming close-set eyes; asked directions, he looks them over past the point of curiosity or mere ill manners. Why is this cretin so damned nosy? But before he can be challenged, the man straightens, turns, and points, barking harsh syllables over his shoulder as he hurries off down the night street.

AFTER OSWIECIM'S JEWS were transported to the Cracow ghetto, their houses were occupied by Christians, that snoop's forebears doubtless among them. And the girl's family, too, perhaps, in their old "Yittish" house. Were you young people never told, he says, that after the war, when those few returning refugees made their way back home to Poland to reclaim their lives, they were reviled and driven off and sometimes bludgeoned and occasionally, when too persistent, killed? "Nearly two thousand Jews were murdered in this country *after* the war," he says. "Didn't you know that?"

"Murtered?" They have stopped their fooling. They look shocked—less by the statistic, he suspects, than by their passenger's intensity. "No, sir! Sorry! We were never learned such things!"

"Why sorry? You weren't born yet." His tone is too dismissive: the boy's regret had been sincere. "At home, at school is what I meant."

Mirek is silent. The two heads in the front seat, facing

forward, seem hypnotized by the *thwack-wack-wack-thwack* of ragged windshield wipers dragged across cold muddied glass.

Why challenge them that way, idiot? What did you expect? He scowls in the same instant that his scowl is caught by the boy's scared eyes in the rearview mirror, reading the stranger's expression the wrong way.

FAR FROM BEING ISOLATED in some grim landscape, as postwar newsreels led one to imagine, the high-fenced compound, now a state museum, is located between thoroughfares at the edge of town. Though night has come, the gate into its forecourt is untended, open to the street, and the black wrought ironwork of the gate arch, gleaming in the rain, is still in place a half century later.

Frantic to be of use, the girl pieces out the sign: "Is meaning, 'Verk Make Frei'!" And the boy hushes her. "You are okay, mister?"

Mirek has slowed to a near stop as the little car approaches the gate, but his passenger waves him on through. All three look back over their shoulders, as if that portal, left unwatched, might close silently behind.

The night court is empty. A two-story building on the

far side of the court is outlined by the glare of prison light; its few windows appear lightless. Pulling up short of the entrance, Mirek keeps the motor running. They stare about them, making no move to get out.

In a voice gone hoarse, the passenger inquires, "How do you feel? Being here, I mean? How does it feel to come to such a place? In your own country?" The young Poles exchange looks of alarm. Why would their guest ask them such a thing so many years after those shrouded times that even the old people claim they can scarcely remember?

He presses them. Hadn't they noticed that old railway embedded in the road? Surely they knew that before those first transports of Jews arrived from western Europe, thousands of Polish prisoners had already been exterminated in this place—*your own damned people, boys and girls*, he wants to yell, *right here behind these walls! Wake up!*

When they answer at last, they speak in whispers. They say, It was too long ago. They say, We cannot even imagine it. They say, We don't know how to think about something so incredible—not, he notes, "so terrible" but "so incredible," so far beyond belief, as if no sane intelligence could comprehend, far less accept, that such enormous horror could take place in this quiet neighborhood of the girl's hometown.

She is sniffling. Mirek jumps out, wrenches open the door, yanks out the scuffed valise by its leather straps. They want him gone. He tries in vain to compensate them for the petrol, entreats the girl to at least accept with his sincere best wishes this bit of amber she had liked so much in Cracow. "Please, please, sir," she whispers, tears in her eyes. "Is beauty gift for Mama!"

They depart at once, leaving him alone with his father's suitcase, his spurned amber. When the little car scoots through the gate, the petal of the girl's pale face appears in her blurred window, and he lifts his hand in a half wave— all there is time for. The little auto flees up the empty avenue, tires whistling on the wet pavement. Couldn't those kids have waited long enough to make sure the guest of Poland had been let in?

Not that he'd deserved much courtesy. They had been kind to lug him thirty miles on a winter road to this *cloaca maxima*, and he had repaid them with pedantic hectoring and pried at them with an irritable meanness that he cannot blame on jet lag or fatigue, or not entirely. *What is it, then? You damn well better pull yourself together.*

Hearing something, or perhaps not, he whirls to confront the dark building behind him, relieved to find the heavy door outlined with light. Eventually it opens at his rapping and a woman, finger to her lips, urges his silence. This is the former admissions building, yes. He'd been expected earlier.

He eats a plate of leftover cold fare alone in the SS mess hall, windowless and tomb-walled as a subway station; he follows big red arrows up a steep sharp-cornered stair to an SS dormitory converted to cramped quarters for those few visitors with reason to stay the night fifty years later. A corridor with scaling paint leads to a narrow room where a man occupying one of the twin cots rolls over and feigns sleep to spare them both the toil of introductions.

A casement window overlooks the inner compound. Shards of fractured light expose silhouettes of regimented barracks, hard-edged as a prison on a stage set. At the far end of this street—or so he is presently advised by a voice that erupts in phlegmy coughs behind him—stands the former residence of the late commandant of SS Konzentrationlager Auschwitz I, handy to the gallows site of his postwar hanging.

His informant has twitched his sheet aside, baring a mouth red as a wound that splits the stubble on a long Scandinavian face. "Why do you stare, if I may ask? You never see a Nordic Jew before?" Upon which this visage with its crafty leer is withdrawn under the blanket, together with a muffled snort he thinks might have been laughter.

He lies there travel-spent, unable to sleep, much closer than he likes to that alien male body on the other cot. The oppression seeping from these walls, he thinks, can only be deepened by his own misgivings as to why he has come here in the first place, together with his dread of the next days. His fault, of course. But what has he gotten himself into?

"You really have no choice about it, do you?" his step-mother had said. "No," he'd said, still gazing at that photo. "Not anymore." Then, very quietly, she'd said, "Your father had no choice about it either, yet he never went. Why do I suspect that's the reason the poor guy did it?"

THREE

In the mess hall next morning, over hard dark bread with margarine and worn-out coffee, he is caught up on the mission of this retreat by his roommate, Dr. Anders Stern, the "Nordic Jew" with the long loony face. Altogether, Stern explains, some one hundred and forty pilgrims from twelve countries have committed themselves to a week of homage, prayer, and silent meditation in memory of this camp's million and more victims, and "through personal testimony," reads the manifesto, "to bear witness lest the world forget man's depthless capacity for evil if such horror is to be diminished in the future."

A primatologist and evolutionary biologist with strong opinions on the fatal role of the human species on the tree of life, Anders Stern is one of those perverse intellectuals who enjoy the role of the buffoon. He wears wool britches with suspenders and a peasant's rubber knee boots and a big manure-hued overshirt. Blue eyes, pale hair set off oddly by black brows; deep furrow lines between those eyes as in the scowls of primitives; that wet red mouth with the out-thrust lower lip that ensures a not quite comic air of grievance. He speaks more loudly than he needs to, over-talks others, interrupts. Belching noisily out of habit, he declares he is attending this retreat in the hope that in all-day silent meditation in a death camp, he might arrive at some insight on mass sadism that could cast light on the evolutionary purpose of so-called human evil—

"*So-called* evil, you say?" a woman's voice complains. "Evolutionary *purpose?*"

Listening to Stern at the mess hall tables are a number of retreatants, mostly middle-aged and older people, humbly spoken and uncomfortable when noticed. Many are practiced in the silent meditation that is the organizing principle of this retreat and all have at least a scraped acquaintance with the English language. The majority, Stern informs his roommate a bit loudly, are Jews and Christians from Israel, the United States, and Western Europe, most of them German; others include a young Palestinian and a makeshift Tibetan Buddhist from New Jersey named O'Brien. "Unaffiliated" is a Mr. G. Earwig, no indicated nationality, and last-minute arrangements have been made for a late arrival, Dr. D. Clements Olin, Polish-born American poet and scholar, who is not formally enrolled but has attached himself to this retreat to take advantage of the economy of these lean accommodations and their proximity and access to the camp itself.

Dr. Olin is duly introduced by Stern to the retreat's unofficial "spiritual leader," nicknamed Ben Lama, a genial, bearded, near-bald psychologist left over from the flower-power days of a psychedelic California youth ("Master of Tibetan Tantra and ex-hippie ex–Orthodox Jew," snorts Anders Stern, who is much amused by the ecumenical mix here from America).

At university in Massachusetts, Clements Olin had immersed himself in the literature of the Third Reich and the Shoah. Eventually, he'd been appointed full professor of twentieth-century Slavic literature, with emphasis on its great modern poets—Akhmatova, Herbert, Milosz, Szymborska—and a special interest in the survivor texts; he is presently completing a monograph on Tadeusz Borowski for a university press.

Although he is offered readings and lectureships in Warsaw and is well-traveled elsewhere in Europe, this journey to his native region never seemed to come about until this year, when his father's sudden death was followed closely by word from his meditation group in Cambridge, notifying practitioners about a pioneer retreat in the winter. Suddenly, with mixed feelings, he was on his way—not "going home to Poland," he assured his friends and colleagues, no, no, certainly not. True, he would be passing through his ancestral region while completing research on the role of death camps in the work of the ambiguous Borowski, doomed author of the brilliant, controversial *This Way for the Gas, Ladies and Gentlemen*. Indeed, half the weight strapped into his father's old valise consists of research notes and outlines, early drafts, paperback volumes of the literature, also galley proofs of a new collection of those excellent Slav poets edited by D. Clements Olin, Ph.D. (His Borowski monograph is not the only reason he has come, but he sees no point in mentioning the other, which he considers sentimental or at least too personal, too likely to invite the wrong sort of attention.) He is here as a researcher, he informs Ben Lama. As a stranger in Poland, with no close family lost in the war, he has no authentic witness to contribute and will probably stay only two or three days.

"A researcher." Ben Lama nods slowly twice or thrice before murmuring, "I see." Though he says it pleasantly enough, his "I see" seems a bit cryptic to Olin, perhaps even a mild rebuke, and who could blame the man? With immense archives of evidence and testimony so readily available, Ben must be thinking, what sort of "research" can be left for this poor fool to do? What could his research possibly contribute that has not, long since, with lacerating eloquence, been flayed upon the page?

Olin tends to agree with the many who have stated that fresh insight into the horror of the camps is inconceivable, and efforts at interpretation by anyone lacking direct personal experience an impertinence, out of the question; in the words of the survivor-writer Aharon Appelfeld, "The Holocaust belongs to the type of enormous experience that reduces one to silence. Any utterance, any statement, any 'answer' is tiny, meaningless, and occasionally ridiculous. Even the greatest of answers seems petty." He will never pierce through to the "something incredible" mentioned by that boy Mirek, to that twisted black shrunken "coil of evil" cited by Poland's great Yiddish writer I. B. Singer. So what can he hope to understand here? He would never dare attempt to name it even if he could imagine such a thing, a bead of illumination glimpsed from a poet's oblique angle, some fleeting *apprehension* which might clarify, for example, the enigma of Borowski's abrupt suicide at age twenty-eight, at the pinnacle of his celebrity and just three days after the birth of his first child to his longtime lover.

ON THIS FIRST MORNING a film documentary made by the liberating armies will be followed by a guided tour of this base camp, Auschwitz I; in the afternoon and for the next five days, all day in every weather, the retreatants will trek the long mile across the fields to the extermination camp KL Vernichtungslager Auschwitz II to offer prayer at its gas chambers and crematoria and all-day silent meditation on the long railway ramp known as "the selection platform."

Although Professor Olin is not registered as a participant, he is experienced in meditation practice, and Ben Lama invites him to join the retreat schedule, coming and going as he pleases. This morning, he forgoes the screening on a strong instinct to confront the death camp all alone on this first day, undistracted by the dismay of others.

LEAVING AUSCHWITZ I, he crosses the main railroad tracks, following directions to the outlying farmland community known as Brzezinka, "The Birches"—in German, Birkenau. Years before, Olin's father had described to him this countryside he knew well as a boy and later as a young cavalry lieutenant, the army stables and broad pastures, the farms, orchards, and shaded lanes of its quaint hamlets.

Not until 1940, as reported by Borowski, were those communities razed to create a buffer zone around the camp, with the inhabitants presumably resettled in the confiscated houses of the Jews.

Beyond the tracks, he follows an ice-puddled dirt road through the fields, along a ditch line of hard-cropped winter trees. In the distance, delicate as netting, high fences drift forth through a brownish fog. Soon the hazy outline of the main sentry tower thrusts up from a red wall of end-to-end brick buildings, slapped up in haste in 1942, Borowski wrote, by Russian prisoners from the eastern front before they perished of starvation. Below the tower, like the mouth of an ogre's cave, an arched railway tunnel bores through the prison walls into the impoundment.

Uneasy, he enters by a broken gate and ventures through. Where the tunnel opens out into the camp, the railway splits into three tracks served by parallel ramps that separate two vast barbed-wired enclosures. Where these platforms draw to a point and end, pale ruins like immense mushrooms lie half-hidden in thin woods.

On the north side, in its own fenced compound possibly a mile across, stand the foundations of what is left of the small city of old stables used as barracks for male prisoners, long ramshackle sheds with black earth floors and missing slats and myriad chinks open to the weather. All but the sheds nearest the entrance had been burned down at war's end by the Red Army, leaving a wasteland of charred chimneys like black stumps in the wake of forest fire.

Vast emptiness, terminal silence, under a gray overcast withholding snow. "Bearing witness"? Dear God. In the echo of such desolation, what more witness could be needed? *Vernichtungslager. Extermination camp.* The name signified all by itself a mythic barbarism and depravity.

Could there be seasons in this place or is it always winter? He could be breathing the air of the Dark Ages.

Reading Borowski was Olin's first exposure to the swarming scenes of terror on this platform, the howls of lost children running everywhere and nowhere "like wild dogs," the young mother so frantic to be spared that she forsakes the little boy calling *Mama! Mama!* who runs behind her ("Oh no, sir! He's not mine!"), casting away the last of her humanity for a few more hours of excruciating life. Who could hear the despair of that child, the cries of all those children being stripped of their brief moment on this earth, without suffering this urge that he feels now, a half century too late, to beat and kick those dolled-up SS pigs into a jelly—

Stop! To rage this way over dead history is ludicrous. Among the participants in this retreat, the several sons and daughters of defunct SS may well be the most agonized of all, and their ordeal will be stark enough without the unearned indignation of some damned onlooker from abroad who has no connection to the place and no meaningful witness to contribute.

He has faltered, needing to compose himself, find his breath before proceeding. But when he starts forward with intent to walk the platform all the way to those half-hidden ruins in the woods, he stops again almost at once, feeling somehow threatened. In a moment, he retreats, edging backward into the tunnel mouth like some night creature in response to a dim instinct not to expose itself outside its lair.

⋇

CLEMENTS OLIN is not sorry to have missed the film, having seen enough of that grim footage elsewhere; the last time, numb, he had shifted in his seat every few moments to rouse himself to his moral duty and absorb more punishment. He'd felt ashamed. But even horror becomes wearisome, and by now every adult in the Western world has been exposed to awful images of stacked white corpses and body piles bulldozed into pits—no longer human beings, simply *things*, not nearly as shocking as a photo from the SS archives of two live wild-haired women crying out through the small barred window of their cattle car. Crying out to whom? Their fellow men? Perhaps this fellow man taking their picture? In the absence of their God, who could have heard them, let alone set them free?

Images of howling victims protesting insane fate had always horrified him more than those apparitions clutching at barbed wire, too far gone even to grasp that these rough figures outside the fence, pointing cameras at their pitiful condition as children might point fingers in a zoo, are the saviors prayed for throughout thousands of hours, day and night and night and day for months and years until prayers guttered in their throats and their eyes stared in the way they would in death.

THE GUIDED TOUR after the film has been slow in getting started; by the time he returns, his companions have only just entered the museum, moving slowly up the stair to the exhibits on the second floor. He trails after them, but on the landing he hangs back to avoid the droning of the guide (who reminds him not agreeably of that seedy local who had peered too long into Mirek's car the night before).

Hunched in his cocoon of statistics, the guide moves sniffing through the midden heaps of humble things—grayed toothbrushes, tins of cracked shoe polish, tangles of wire spectacles, their old-fashioned round lenses broken out or missing, all protected behind walls of glass. From whom? What breed of scavenger would pilfer such sad stuff?

Needlessly—senselessly, he thinks—the guide identifies these objects. This big pile of little shoes, he rasps, contains two thousand pairs removed from the killed children. "So who was counting?" an American complains under his breath. Nobody smiles but none look offended, either. Nobody knows whom to be angry with in such a place, unless it's these mute Germans with warm breakfast in their guts who stand among them. Afraid of glancing at a German by mistake, they look straight ahead, glaring at nothing.

The nagging is monotone, mechanical—the voice of a tour guide in Hades, Olin thinks: *Over here, please, ladies? You are please looking over here? Is grand scenic attraction! Is world-famous River Styx!*

And there it is, oh Christ, the hair. Hacked from the heads of mothers, lovers, daughters, whole bins of it, like dusty heaps of ancient hay left behind by war.

Feeling faint, he touches the wall to find his balance. He knows his resentment of the guide is no more reasonable than his rage last night at the local guy at the car window. Still, this little rat might at least inform these people that because human hair resists the damp, whole bales were harvested for the manufacture of winter garments and coat linings, even sofa stuffing for the further comfort of heavily upholstered German asses. The display includes hideous sweaters spun for wartime consumers in the Fatherland:

How were such items labeled in the shops? Would knowledge of their origin have discouraged sales among pious
German Christians? Was there no moral disapproval, no
distaste for their vile provenance, no tremor of foreboding?
No squeamishness about "Jew hair" from "Jew bodies," the
last residue of despised Jewishness? Pulling these sweaters
on over their heads, had they held their breath to spare
themselves queer Hebrew odors?

He emits a gasp that the others, all eyes to the front, take
great pains not to notice. Oh Lord. Hadn't Borowski and
the rest discovered in the end that rage and bitterness, not
to speak of vengeful fantasies, were only different prisons?
And unlike many of these Europeans, he had suffered no
hardship in the war and has nothing, really, to complain of;
he cannot even claim he missed his mother, having never
known her.

So where is all this indignation coming from? It seems
so unlike the man he thought he knew, the urbane, soft-
spoken Clements Olin, academic poet and historian, cultured, multilingual, dryly ironic (a rather dark humor, some
might complain), and on occasion moody and volatile
enough to be thought "interesting." Divorced and child-
less, he has been prey most of his life to loneliness and
nameless melancholy—well? who hasn't?—which he keeps
to himself where it belongs. Even so, he holds fast to the
hope that one day he might remarry somebody with chil-

dren (well-mannered, of course, and unobtrusive) though well aware that, at fifty-five, the day grows late.

FOOTSTEPS ON the bare wood floor resound too loudly. A stifled cry and many weep. Still, they do not look at one another. Like the first sinners fleeing Paradise in a medieval painting, hands clasped to their errant genitals, they cannot in this moment face the shame they see reflected in the eyes of other human beings.

At the exit, the guide turns toward him, the better to draw attention to his truancy. Awaiting the laggard, the herd stands stupefied, like cattle at the gate. Olin, approaching, inquires in Polish, "You're a local man, are you? From Oswiecim?" Though the man nods, his silence is sullen to the point of rudeness. He knows he has not been questioned but accosted.

IN THE

OGRE'S CAVE

FOUR

Outside, all huddle in the cold, awaiting entry to the camp itself. On this December morning of soot-dirtied snow, the grainy air tastes bitter. A gray scene with harsh black outlines as in old news clips of the camps, as if with the extinguishing of life, the last colors had drained away into the earth.

The compound with its rigid rows of two-story red-brick blocks looks much as it had in prewar days when it served as a harvest labor camp, then a military barracks. After the Occupation, in 1939, it was reconstituted as a holding camp for some ten thousand "élites," or educated Poles—intellectuals, aristocrats, artists, military officers, and other potential dissidents and leaders, categories that would certainly have included Olin's father, the young cavalry lieutenant, and his grandparents, too, had they not escaped abroad.

In the barracks, in SS photos on the wall, white clustered faces peer out from their shelves like families of opossums from their holes. Along the corridor hang stylized photo portraits of prisoners shorn bald—the handiwork, Olin supposes, of some sensitive fascist of artistic inclination. In bewilderment and fear, dark-shadowed sleepless eyes stare out of bony falcon sockets. ("If the Germans win the war," Borowski wrote, "how will the world ever find out about what happened to us?")

In Block 10 were administered the assorted sadisms of "experimental medicine." Block 11, called "the Death Block," housed the quest for efficient methods of mass "roach" extermination. In its basement are cramped torture cells: the Darkness Cell, the Standing Cell. In the Hunger Cell, a fresh candle is offered by two Catholic novices in black street habit, faces half-lit in the chiaroscuro of the dungeon darkness.

"What's that, some kind of a damned altar?" The loud, sudden voice is just outside the thronged cell door.

Eyes closed, palms together, calm, the candle lighter raises her fingertips to her chin and her younger companion, frightened, does the same. "For Saint Maximilian, sir," the candle lighter answers softly without turning, "who offer his own life—"

"'—to save a fellow prisoner, a family man,' correct? The Myth of Auschwitz!"

The brutal voice in this cramped space scrapes Olin's nerves. *"Hey!"* he shouts as if silencing a dog, hating his own rude intrusion. The novices stare from one shouter to the other. "Earwig," Anders whispers.

The man's eyes squint, his nostrils flare. He meets Olin's glare for a long moment before turning to ape the consternation of a Polish priest who stands nearby, pale hands half-raised in protest. When the priest won't engage him, he turns on the novices again. "You holy Romans don't belong here, girls." The junior nun looks stunned, on the point of tears; the candle lighter stills her with firm fingers on her forearm. The priest says nothing. He is a husky man with a blue jaw that will always need a shave, but his eyes look broken and his mouth uncertain, and his skin is glazed by perspiration even in the cold. (When he thanks Olin later for speaking up to defend the novices, Olin says brusquely, "All I said was *Hey*." What he wanted to say was, *Where in hell were you?*)

Ben Lama says mildly, *"Everyone* belongs here. These sisters are very welcome." Having noticed Olin's agitation, he signals to him to let the whole thing pass. "Take nothing personally, Dr. Olin," he advises sotto voce. "Not this week."

THE PROTOTYPE GAS CHAMBER and crematorium at Auschwitz I is located in a bunker mound camouflaged by a knoll of scraggy pines; the guide points out what he claims are the faint claw marks made by human finger bones on the concrete ceiling. On the wall of a brick building opposite the mound, a wire mesh enclosing seed and suet is visited by quick blue tits. Who is it, Olin wonders, who sets out winter food for little birds in such a place?

Watching the bird feeder, Olin grows aware that he is being watched by the older novice, the one chastised for offering that candle; intercepted, her gaze holds for a moment, flicks away.

The cul-de-sac between Blocks 10 and 11 is blocked at the far end by the Black Wall: the heavy wood used in its construction, says the guide, nodding gravely out of deep respect for his inside knowledge, had to be replaced with concrete after the wood was shot to splinters. In the first years, thirty to forty thousand people, mostly Poles, were executed here; he points out gutters along the base of the side walls that channeled all that inferior Slav blood down rusty drains.

At the Black Wall, candles and incense are offered to the martyred as voices rise in Kaddish, the Prayer for the Dead, in which the Lord and all his works are glorified.

("Death camps included?" The hoarse whisper is ignored.)

May the Great Name be exalted and sanctified in the
world that He created according to His will and may
His kingdom reign in your lifetime and in your days
and in the lifetime of the house of Israel. And say,
Yes, Amen.

The sacred text is read aloud in the original Aramaic and in Hebrew, then murmured in the half dozen languages of this convocation. A young man named Rainer, Ben Lama's retreat assistant from Berlin, recites forcefully in his native tongue, unaware how his harsh Teutonic intonations might grate upon the ears of mostly Jewish listeners.

The agonized sound of the ram's horn blown before and after Kaddish is man's last cry of protest against his fate, a glum American rabbi called James Glock instructs them. Of all sounds, the shofar is the loneliest, says Rabbi Glock. It is the voice of the living calling out prayer across the void to the nameless, numberless dead who do not answer. In Olin's mind, it awakens a memory of a huge pumpkin collapsing in upon itself in an October field in the New England dusk, a sight that had struck him in boyhood as the loneliest thing he'd ever seen.

Above the Wall, thin black branches of the naked birches flail the gray overcast like exposed nerves. "You too?" a young Frenchman whispers, noticing Olin's fixed expression. "This accursed air? We breathe in, *n'est-ce pas?* But nothing is coming out." Olin nods politely. He has no comfort to offer.

AUSCHWITZ I, with its upstairs museum, is all most visitors, descending for a quick half day from their round-trip charter bus from Cracow, might feel inclined to see; he imagines them reeling back aboard, undone by so much evidence of huge cold crimes. But Ben Lama's would-be witness bearers are no tourists, and neither are they Holocaust voyeurs come to indulge a morbid curiosity; most seem to be here on painful missions incompletely understood, by themselves perhaps least of all. By the look of them, some must have sacrificed savings and vacations to travel here from other countries. Many had relatives among the victims, Ben Lama says; others are stricken descendants of the "perpetrators." One shocked woman has collapsed and must be helped back to her room, but she soon sends word that she intends to see this through: she will not retreat to Cracow and fly home.

"That's the choice," Ben Lama comments publicly at the noon meal. "We pass through quickly, sickened and depressed, or we stay for days and sit with it in meditation; we immerse ourselves and are transformed—" Here he stops short, grinning sheepishly as the wave of his own rhetoric overtakes him. "Anyway," he smiles, "that's our game plan for the next few days."

Olin trusts this man's wry tone and absence of pretension. Respecting the good intentions of the others, he resolves to suppress a wince at sentimental rubbish about "closure" and "healing" and "confronting the Nazi within," or when this gathering is referred to as a "spiritual retreat": what "spiritual" business can these people have here? What transcendence do they aspire to, hope to attain? (And come to that, how "spiritual" had many of the victims been before their martyrdom? Surely a few in every transport had been cruel greedy bastards, never much missed at home.)

As for "bearing witness," the term strikes his ear as anachronistic and over-earnest. Excepting the few elderly survivors among them, what meaningful witness can any of them bear so many years after the fact? Witness to *what*, exactly? The emptiness? That silence? What can they hope to offer besides prayer in belated atonement for the guilt of absence, of having failed to share in unimaginable sufferings? Or hope to experience in this dead place beyond unearned gratification of shallow spiritual ambition? Their mission here, however well-intended, is little more than a wave of parting to a ghostly horror already withdrawing into myth.

Not that he questions their sincerity. But who among them, Clements Olin included, has truly understood the conclusion of Borowski, Primo Levi, and others: that no one in the death camps, not even the victims, was wholly innocent of what was perpetrated here or wholly different from the perpetrators? Hadn't all participants been compromised if only as members of a species capable of such cruelty? Perhaps only the occupants of those small shoes had died unstained.

So even if these companions witness truly, what could "truly" mean? Spreading word of their impressions of this scene of heinous crime? Too late, too late. There had been so many such scenes, so many million crimes. Anyway, as he teaches in his classes, humankind has known forever what needed to be done to bring its own propensities under control, yet whole millennia of civilizations and religions and ever more complex scientific knowledge, all that striving with its high purpose and beautiful accomplishment, has not sufficed to tame the inner beast even a little. On the contrary, the first half of this century was surely the most villainous in recorded history, if only in sheer numbers of human lives systematically destroyed by human beings. Surely the time, means, and good will of would-be "witness bearers" might be better spent out in the world, helping the hordes of refugees and other sufferers for whom some sort of existence might yet be salvaged. The point of life is to help others through it—who said that?

We must help the living while we can, since the dead have no more need of us.

In this empty place then, in winter, 1996, what was left to be illuminated? What could the "witness" of warm, well-fed visitors possibly signify? How could such "witness" matter and to whom? No one was listening.

LACKING WINDOWS, the mess hall is oppressive, and the noon meal is mostly silent; in the aftershock of the first morning, the crash of heavy white crockery in the steel sinks subdues the few feeble conversations, all but one insistent female voice. Over her cold hard sausage, hard potato, stiff black bread, an American woman in a fur-lined leather coat is complaining that nothing had prepared her for anything so terrible as this morning, not even that movie about the kind German enamel manufacturer in Cracow who saved his whole list of productive employees, a team of lovable Jews. "It made me want to run right out," she cried, "and *do* something for those people!"

At a nearby table, Earwig rounds on her like a poked badger. "*Do* something, lady?" he snarls. "Like what? Take a Jew to lunch?"

"You're horrible!" she protests. "You don't belong on a spiritual retreat!"

Her antagonist stabs an underboiled potato and hoists and inspects it on his fork, thereby somehow conveying his opinion that her damned movie was exploitative and her distress irrelevant. When Ben Lama sighs and rises slowly to approach his table, Earwig is already on his feet on his way out of the room.

⁂

THAT NEED TO EXPERIENCE the silence of the death camp undistracted still unsatisfied, Olin sets out for Birkenau again directly after the noon meal. This time, knowing others will be coming, he enters the cavernous mouth of the arched gate—the Ogre's cave, he thinks oddly, the cave of Glob the Ogre—and passes quickly through the tunnel, raising his hood to fend off a cold wind as he emerges in the camp and sets out toward the crematoria.

He has not gone far when, despite himself, he glances back toward the tunnel. No one. What he sees instead, emerging slow as a horse turd from that orifice, is the snout of a locomotive and with it the shriek of iron he'd first heard crossing the Cracow road, as if that phantom transport through the forest were just now arriving, a half century late.

Far down the platform, a figure stands facing the woods. Leaving the mess hall before the meal was finished, that scold of the young nuns had come straight here. When Olin approaches and attempts to pass, the man barks *"Hey!"* in mocking imitation of Olin's shout earlier this morning, then steps into his path, hiking a bristled chin at him in a street challenge.

The unshaven G. Earwig is squat, round-shouldered, compact—a build Olin associates with city cabbies and cigar store proprietors, thickset short men with loud hoarse ballpark voices. His mouth is hard-set in a short sardonic smile that never widens, and his eyes stay all but hidden by thick lids. Black leather cap, black pants, black leather jacket bulked by dirty-looking sweaters, he looks like Olin's idea of an old-time revolutionary, a veteran of some lost cause, hard, cold, remote.

The man clears his throat and spits. "The Polack Holocaust authority, right? You here to write about it?" He waves his hand to indicate the vast dimensions of the camp. "Think you can handle it?" Earwig's eyes have a disconcerting way of rolling back in disbelief, baring too much white, as if he'd been struck blind. "You got some new angle on mass murder, maybe, that ain't been written up yet in maybe ten thousand fucking books?"

Olin turns on him so abruptly—*"What?"*—that the other actually steps back, raising half-closed fists. Feeling foolish, Olin shoves his own hands into his parka pockets. "Okay, calm down," he says. "I'm not qualified to write about it. I wouldn't know where to begin."

"You know that much anyway." Having already lost interest, Earwig turns toward the tunnel, where others are starting to appear. "So what are you people really up to? What are you kibitzers really here for?"

Olin ignores this, stepping around him to avoid some grotesque showdown: *Pissed-Off Trippers Duke It Out on Platform Where Millions Died!* Mock tabloid headlines have always amused him, and when he does not bother to hide a little grin, the man shouts at him again. But this time his *"Hey!"* is a parody of his own shouting, and he thrusts out a thick hand and a growled name, Somebody Earwig.

Still in bad temper, Olin stalls, in no hurry to accept the proffered hand. *"Georgie,* you said? Sorry. Gyorgi, maybe?" For despite that New York City voice, the man seems distinctly European.

Earwig doesn't answer. "So I was too rough on those nuns, you think?" He nods when Olin nods. "Yeah, probably. But Kolbe?" He is off again. "And fucking Pius? And this Polack pope they got in there now trying to sanctify those Jew-haters!"

Despite his mistrust of the Vatican, Olin is offended: he has never heard a Jewish friend or colleague speak of the ancient enemy with such contempt. Why is that? he once inquired. Maybe because we're still outnumbered, his friend joked, finessing an argument doomed to go nowhere.

Earwig nods as if Olin's discomfort was precisely his intent. "Okay, okay," he says. "But what I heard, we got one of their sick priests here with us. Somebody at the convent passed the word. Next thing you know, he'll be corrupting one of our nice ecumenicals."

There are several priests attending this retreat. Olin doesn't take the bait by asking the man's name, in fact says nothing.

Now that travel to Poland is possible again, says Earwig, already off in a new direction, it's only a matter of time before "outings" such as this retreat become an industry. "This year it's crummy room and board in the old SS quarters in winter: next year, new dorms, Jewish school groups, spring seminars, conventions. Then come your package tours and jumbo buses, youth hostels, snack bars, kosher fast food, souvenir tchotchkes—the whole matzoh ball. And See Historic Auschwitz postcards: *Awesome, man! Check it out! Signed, Yr pal, Schlomo.*"

Olin's smile is sour and Earwig grunts, fed up with wasting his inspired spleen on such an audience. He surveys the half-mile ramp. "Ever seen those cattle cars?" He'd seen one as a kid, early in the war. "Stuck on a railroad siding. Hot, hot, hot, no air, no water. Jesus! I mean, how long had those people *been* there?"

"Probably kids in there, too," Olin agrees.

"No good sniveling over little shoes. Got to hear 'em

shuffling along this platform, smell their rotten little socks. Got to *smell* 'em, man! Smell their dead breath right there where you're standing. You got to *feel* those people."

"The way you do, right?"

Earwig turns on him, suspicious. "Hell no, I can't feel 'em! Not in that kick-in-the-balls way I'm talking about. And you can't either, pal. So you better just set your ass down on this platform and 'become one' with their suffering along with your Zen buddies over there." He is suddenly incensed. "You people are amazingly full of shit, you know that?"

Olin walks off before his own anger gets away from him. "Keep talking, Georgie," he calls over his shoulder. "Just keep shooting your damned mouth off and maybe you'll be all right."

Certainly he had not meant to suggest that he himself had any special insight. In fact, his vision of the locomotive emerging from the tunnel mouth has scared him. What if, in the coming days, his identity should be subsumed into a horde of doomed humanity milling and bumping around him on this platform? Not those blurred figures in the SS photos, those bulky shapes in dark overcoats with white blanks for faces but real live sweating human beings with real voices still remembered in real communities back home? What if here at the terminus, the final destination, his feelings laid open by this silence, he no longer experiences the victims as ciphers separate from himself, but as terrified creatures clamoring for water and some word about their whereabouts or destination, still clinging to the hope of life on this long ramp that led from the sane world they thought they knew straight into hellfire and the void?

In the image that disturbed him most among the thousands he has studied, a young mother, staggering in summer heat under her load of winter clothing, shrieks at her three kids. Of different heights, the three are pressed shoulder to shoulder, tight as nestlings, close as ill-matched beads, perhaps more frightened of their mother's howls than of the bored trooper in the background, rifle slung over his shoulder, there to see to it—they don't know this yet—that these despised creatures proceed in good order to their deaths within the hour. Years later, he can still see the dirt smudges on the bare calves of those children, feeling thankful that they stand backs to the camera, scared faces mercifully concealed.

Presumably Tadeusz Borowski witnessed or in some way experienced most of his own frightful scenes. "All of us walk around naked"—that first line of his book—had struck Olin at once as a glimpse of genius.

"Vorarbeiter Tadeusz," he called his narrator, who is also addressed by the author's nickname. Had the real "Tadek" survived here only as a *Vorarbeiter*, a privileged facilitator of the dirty work? Otherwise why give that name to his hard-nosed, cynical, but also horrified anti-hero? In guilt and shame? Seemingly, his reader is meant to think so.

　　　　　　　　　　　　✳

EARWIG, OVERTAKING HIM, is plainly indifferent to how unwelcome he has made himself and misreads Olin's expression: "*Who is this morbid Jew sonofabitch shooting his mouth off in my face*—that what you're thinking? *Who needs him?* And so naturally you are pissed off like the others, and maybe you people are right." He holds Olin's eye. "And maybe you're wrong. Think about it. Maybe you're just wandering around out here with your thumb up your ass, waiting for some answer that might let you off the hook. Because you don't know why you're here or what you're looking for, correct?"

Olin says quietly, "I'm not looking for anything. I'm listening. To this silence, I mean."

"That why you came all the way to fucking Poland? To hear silence? Bullshit. You think you'll hear lost voices, right? Like all the rest of 'em." When Olin ignores him, Earwig, exasperated, points at the people straggling behind them. "Look, why don't you just go tag along with all the good guys, Prof? Bear some nice witness or whatever the hell they think they're doing."

"And G. Earwig? What's *he* up to in this place?" Olin demands.

"Who knows? Death camp ghoul, maybe?"

Opposite an entrance into the women's compound, Olin steps down from the ramp onto the tracks. "Look, man, I can't answer your question, and anyway it's none of your damned business." He starts across the tracks, then turns and tries again. "I just needed to come out here by myself, all right? I hadn't thought about the why. Who knows?"

"*Oy! Who knew?*" the other scoffs. "The Holocaust authority, maybe? Unless he doesn't *want* to know—that's another story."

FIVE

On a stretch of platform between tracks where dis-cerning SS doctors selected those few prisoners with enough strength left to be worked to death, the first silent meditation in homage to the dead is being organized. Fur-nished a cushion, Olin joins the oval circle, wondering how well his crossed legs will hold up in the next days; he sits roughly opposite the candle lighter and her companion.

In hooded capes, the nuns perch side by side, as stiff as penguins. The cropped dark hair of the candle lighter, un-covered briefly in adjusting a blue beret, looks oddly wild, as if hacked off without a mirror. Occasionally she writes in a small green notebook, fingertips pinched white at the pen tip like a schoolgirl's. Their eyes meet briefly as she puts her notes away, and since she seems to be the only other person with a notebook, he lifts his own to salute hers, in token of this bond; she looks away and resumes her meditation. She is a rather plain young woman, he decides; it is the intensity of her composure that is interesting.

Following traditional yogic practice, he adjusts his posture, regulates his breath. However, he is restless and his mind soon wanders. From his vantage point in the long oval, looking eastward through high skeins of barbed wire, he can see across the winter fields to a low horizon of rooftops, power lines, a steeple. He will go to Oswiecim to make inquiries, of course, which will come to nothing. It was all too long ago.

LATE IN 1939, fearing arrest by the new Nazi regime in Cracow, Olin's grandparents had prevailed upon their son Alexei, a young lieutenant of the cavalry, to escort them in their flight abroad to England and America. Old Baron Olinski had lugged across the sea into the New World his antique red leather boots denoting his hereditary *schlachta* class (together with the family copy of the *Almanach de Gotha*) and displayed this evidence of Old World status in a glass-topped table in the corner of the modest New World drawing room his British-born Baroness referred to acidly as "the great hall."

Throughout Olin's boyhood, in their small émigré circle, his grandfather had extolled the glories of the ancien régime, all the way back to the old Kingdom of Poland and its grand traditions of religious tolerance, individual freedoms, literature, and music. As refugee expatriates (the term "immigrants" they reserved for the working classes, the so-called Polish-Americans), they reminded one another that for ten centuries their ravaged homeland had been a nation of proud warriors and noble statesmen. Who were the heroes who saved Christian Europe from the Mongol hordes in 1241 and the Islamic empire in 1683 when those heathen Turks were finally driven from Vienna? Hadn't fifteenth-century Poland ruled all Europe from the Baltic east to the Black Sea? Alas, they cried, not once but twice in the centuries since, lawless seizure of her territories by Prussia, Austria, or Russia had erased the Kingdom from the map of Europe. After the first world war she had to be resurrected as a sovereign nation. But Poland's enemies still coveted her mighty grainlands, and scarcely a quarter century later, those German criminals and vile Bolsheviks were back, swarming over her borders from east and west, bent on the partition of all Poland between them, and the first step of the dictators had been elimination of the educated "élites"—"our own sort, for a start," said the old

Baron. The plan was to diminish the average intelligence of a whole people on the cold theory that the decadent West would never come to the defense of hordes of leaderless illiterates in a vast backward hinterland too amorphous and uncivilized to be taken seriously as an independent nation. The campaign of denigration used derisive propaganda— Polish cavalry charging German tanks was a great favorite— including "Polish jokes" (much enjoyed, it is said, by Der Führer himself) that mocked the alleged native ignorance and stupidity. Inevitably such jokes spread to the U.S.: he had heard the term "dumb Polack" used in his own house, where slurs against "Polish-Americans"—those with no intention of returning—were cheerfully tolerated.

On occasion these "expatriots," as his father called the old Baron's inner circle, would fairly shout at "Alexei's boy," so concerned were they for his political education. Hadn't those Red barbarians ("Drunken rapists to a man, I'm told," sniffed the Baroness, with an uneasy lifting and shifting of old hips in her stiff chair) gobbled up all central Europe, burying centuries of history and culture under the hideous concrete of their vassal states? And once again these down-at-heel patricians would invoke the persecution of their class by ancient enemies, never omitting hairbreadth escapes, all those close shaves that drew closer with each telling, like the starving wolves that pursued their sleighs across the Baltic snows in dead of winter.

PERHAPS SIX MONTHS after their arrival in the U.S., Olin's grandparents had heard from their estate agent in Poland a disturbing rumor about a baby boy. Confronted, Olin's father had confessed to a liaison with a young schoolteacher in Oswiecim. Though his story wavered, Alexei seemed to be saying they'd been secretly engaged, and furthermore that he'd urged her to flee with him, but alas, his headstrong Emi, unwilling to forsake her aging parents and a younger sister, had refused.

"But of course she refused!" snapped the Baroness. "I recall that girl! She had real spirit! She had character!" And she peered down her long nose at her son, who looked injured but said nothing. Subsequently, of course, the old lady would adjust her recollections and decry the disgraceful morals of "that little trollop," the lack of breeding evident at once to any but a lovesick idiot, in short her son, who in addition to his other defects and shortcomings, it appeared, had ignobly abandoned the unwed mother of his unborn child.

As Alexei himself would complain in later life, the old Baron had protested his wife's disparagement, not of their son but of that pretty Emi. Living in Silesia, ruled formerly by Austria, her family like his own spoke German, having long ago adopted the Hapsburg culture of Prague and Vienna: that girl, he declaimed, was "not some peasant wench for a young wastrel to wrong without a care!" Her father, Dr. Allgeier (a blond blue-eyed "blockhead," in the opinion of the old Baron) had failed to flee to save his family as the old Baron had so wisely done but instead persisted in his blockheaded intent to live out his life in the old family house outside Oswiecim and pursue his own practice out of his own sunny office, being persuaded that no physician of Prussian heritage and excellent repute would be interfered with by that new regime over in Cracow.

THE COLD of the winter afternoon falls quickly. Toward twilight, as the witness bearers straggle back toward the town, a weak sun, smoggy red, sinks behind the cropped misshapen trees along the road. A woman murmurs that a faint odor of burning flesh still lingers here a half century later, and someone else recalls her mother's account of a woman who had smelled her fate while approaching Oswiecim in the cattle cars. Told she only imagined things, she said, "The smell of my hand passed over a red-hot stove—that is the smell that is coming from this place." But today that odor is no more than the sulfurous pall of low-grade coal descending from the overcast as thick brown fog.

Olin's legs ache from cross-legged meditation in the cold, but as he observes to Anders Stern, any discomfort they might suffer in their good boots and fat parkas, looking forward to warm rooms and a hot supper, is paltry compared to the agonies of the slave prisoners described by Primo Levi on their return along this road from the factory at Monowitz, or Auschwitz III, exhausted and half-frozen in wooden clogs and coarse striped pajama tunics that offered no protection from the weather. What price had the author of *Survival in Auschwitz* paid for what remained of his own life—Levi who seemed so fearful of survival at a fatal cost to others and the consequent lifelong guilt? For many years after he was freed, the Italian writer had reinhabited his former life, recording his ordeal in two tortured, brilliant books, but in the end, or so it seemed, the death camp reclaimed him. In 1987, he destroyed himself—a belated victim, Olin suggests to Dr. Stern, of that fabled "survivor guilt" which one survivor-writer would dismiss as "Holocaust cant."

"Holocaust *cant*?" Anders shakes his unkempt head. Perhaps that writer had felt threatened by the widespread suspicion that survival in a death camp's desperate conditions without betrayal of one's own humanity was impossible for all but a very few. "'We who have come back, we know. The best of us did not return,'" he says, quoting the Viennese survivor Viktor Frankl. *The best of us*—these are the ones who fascinate them both, the ones whose witness was lost before the source of their extraordinary fortitude could be revealed.

The Franciscan sisters would be sure that source was faith, Olin supposes, noticing the two of them along the road. *Faith of our fathers, holy faith, we shall be true to thee 'til death*—the chorus of a hymn sung in the Anglican chapel of the British boarding school to which his family had consigned him soon after the war, at the age of eight. Olin is wondering about faith when Earwig joins them. "Faith?" he jeers. "In Birkenau? Forget it." Olin glances at the novices, wishing to avoid any appearance of fraternizing with their tormentor, but they give no sign that they have noticed anything at all.

In the next days he will ask himself over and over the question that must plague all of them to some degree: Could I have borne it? Could I have endured unceasing fear for even one day, far less a year, without succumbing to base acts of survival-at-any-cost for an extra crust or ladle of thin gruel? He doubts it. Those heroic few, he feels quite sure, would never have included the sheltered Clements Olin. "Know something, Olin?" Anders broods. "Our digestive tract is about all we have in common with those poor doomed bastards."

If the death camp was so terrible, how is it you survived?— the dangerous query, spoken or unspoken, that many survivors were condemned to deal with, as Borowski noted. Dread that others who had known this hell ("known what the fuck they were talking about, unlike us," says Earwig, unconcerned that the novices are still well within earshot) might tolerate one's varnished truth even as they despised it—surely that could help explain why so few had borne honest witness. To immure one's ordeal, to seal one's shame away in some cavity behind the brain, might well have seemed the one way home to one's lost life. Was this, in the end, Anders suggests, what Primo Levi could not manage? And Olin's man Borowski? (For a boisterous man, the Nordic Jew seems rather preoccupied with suicide.)

THE WRUNG-OUT would-be witness bearers, one hundred and forty strong, gather after supper in the small museum auditorium. Ben Lama, opening the meeting, offers the microphone at once to Father Mikal. The priest formally protests this morning's attack on Saint Maximilian Kolbe, the revered Franciscan martyr who offered his own life in exchange for that of another prisoner, a family man, one of ten condemned to death by the SS in a random selection—

"Oh shit, here comes that 'family man' again!" calls Earwig, slouched graceless in his seat. The Vatican had always encouraged the belief that its martyred priest offered

up his life to save some luckless Hebrew: Earwig scoffs at
the absurdity of that idea. "Hell, in those first years most of
the prisoners in Auschwitz I were Poles. Kolbe's 'family
man' was probably another Catholic who hated Jews as
much as he did."

When Father Mikal turns the other cheek, resumes his
seat, Earwig's voice pursues the novices in their retreat toward the door. "Your Polish pope installed his convent
right outside the wall—that's where Christ's little sisters
there are staying. Not your fault, girls," he hollers after
them, "but your convent has no more business in this place
than you do!"

A British clergyman protests, "You say those young
women are not welcome on an ecumenical retreat that pro-
motes a healing of the faiths?"

"*Healing of the faiths?* In a fucking death camp? Never,
my friend. Not ever."

The disgruntled audience turns toward Ben Lama in
hopes he might intervene, perhaps banish this agitator from
their group. Sleepy-eyed Ben merely blinks once, slowly,
watching Earwig settle back into his slouch. And when Ben
rises, it is only to introduce the distinguished Israeli historian and teacher Professor Adina Schreier, a small waistless
woman, all of a piece, whose Art Nouveau necklace of
heavy orange baubles seems to pull her head down and set
it forward in belligerence. Professor Schreier reminds her
audience that the Shoah or Cataclysm or Catastrophe (the

term "Holocaust" merely signifies a burnt offering, she instructs them) is only the most recent of the great persecutions of the Jews and may not be the last. Scapegoats have been essential to autocratic regimes throughout history, and the Roman Church—here she glances at the priest—has been the archenemy of "us Christ-killers" for nearly two thousand years: the Crusades, the Inquisitions, centuries of pogroms and murderous persecutions, culminating in the Shoah. But some of that martyrdom, she says, has been invited by Judaism itself, which in its centuries of struggle to survive without losing its spiritual integrity developed a reclusiveness that aroused suspicion and prejudice, then expedient hate.

"We Jews must recognize our provocation," she suggests provocatively, visibly gratified, even stimulated, when the cluster of Orthodox Jews groans in disapproval.

Earwig again: "Think those nuns were ever told how Hitler's pope sat on his holy hands while Jews by the millions were going up in smoke?"

"Much as I deplore the brutal way you talk, you're not altogether mistaken," Professor Schreier tells him coldly. "But that sort of inflammatory language will get us nowhere."

Ben Lama's raised hand cuts off Earwig's retort: Olin is mildly relieved to see that this amiable man can be tough when he has to be, and that, for whatever reason, Earwig accepts his authority.

THOSE IN DISTRESS are presently encouraged to come up onto the little stage and, using the microphone, to "bear witness" to their own experience. The neediest, most eager speakers are the Germans. ("Me-firsters even in grief, these people," whispers Anders.) Jumping up red in the face, a young man shouts right from his place, so frantic is he to spit up his revulsion after this terrible day.

"AUSCH-vitz iss zo fockink CHERman!" he shouts, throwing his arms wide in the uselessness of his despair. What he especially detests, he says, is the obscene *effici-ence* of this death factory.

"Ja, ja!" a woman agrees, fairly trembling in her hatred of "our German perfectionism." What a great relief it is, she sighs, with a hopeful smile at the closed faces that surround her, to find herself with understanding people who do not regard her as "a German devil."

Olin winces at her premature relief; hearing her speak of it, a few faces set hard and others turn away.

Close to tears, the elderly daughter of a Wehrmacht soldier killed on the Russian front confesses that at the prayer service at the Black Wall this morning, she had dared recite Kaddish in her father's memory.

"Only this most horrible of places permits my heart to speak!" She spreads her arms, baring her heart to the hall, then repeats her countrywoman's mistake, blurting out how grateful she feels to be here bearing witness with all of these good friends from many nations. Again, cold silence.

Several Germans are still struggling with their discovery that beloved menfolk in the family were implicated or worse in "the Final Solution of the Jewish Question." One woman's late poppa turned out to have been an SS guard in this very *Lager*. "Perhaps he was ordered to assist in unspeakable actions," she mourns, starting to sniffle. "And always so kind he was to dogs and children."

A no-nonsense woman from the Netherlands pounces on this cliché. "Jewish dogs, too? Jewish kids? Like our poor little Anne Frank?" Here a soft moan in honor of the young diarist's sacred memory mixes with a groan of disapproval of the unsporting kill. And a voice says, "*Your* little Dutch girl, are you saying? Born in Frankfurt?"

The Dutch woman—big-voiced, with large squarish front teeth—demands to know why the "witness" with the SS man for a father failed to recognize the fascistic propensities of a man who lived under the same roof. How could she have loved so blindly "the kind of man who would take work in Hell"?

"No, no, orders only he obeyed!"

An American cantor, Rabbi Dan, attempts to mediate. Perhaps a child's love for her loving "dad" comes more naturally than mistrust, he pleads, bestowing a gentle smile of blessing and forgiveness on the gathering. After all, weren't

there many like "this lady's dad" who got caught up gradually in a great evil, step by fatal step—

"Goose step by goose step," Earwig barks. "Millions of
goose-stepping *Dummkopf* dads lending their big pink
Christian hands to cold-blooded murder—"

"Mr. Earwig?" Ben's admonition is pitched just above
the hiss of whispers in the hall.

For many years, the German woman continues, she ran
away from the story of her father, who was sent to fight on
the Russian front when still a boy, scarcely sixteen. "He
was victim also!" Badly wounded, he was transferred by
the SS to guard duty at this *Lager*. And she'd come here to
pray he had not done horrible things, "just maybe he help
to hunt some Jewish, maybe put them on trains." She clasps
her hands upon her breast, imploring the silent rows to
understand.

"Poor liddle SS sol-cher poy age of sixteen. He vas victim also!" calls Anders Stern with that loose grin of his, not
malevolent nor intentionally unkind, simply uncouth and
callous—yet it worries Olin that any sort of jibe at their
expense will only further isolate these German people.

SOME OF THE AMERICAN JEWS, Olin supposes, have
come to assuage a secret guilt; some even dare express the

hope that in this place they might experience some inkling of the agonies others had endured while they prospered.

Though her family lost no one in the camps, Awful Miriam, as Anders calls an overdressed American, bemoans her "trauma" on that fateful day when her best friend was "oppressed" by the school bully: he made the "Jew-Jew girl" salute him in his soldier-father's souvenir regalia, the swastika armband and broad black belt and high-peaked eagle cap. No teacher interfered, she mourns, and one even pretended it was all a joke when those jeering kids marched around her friend making "*Heil* Hitler" salutes!

A silence. Earwig rears around to squint at her. "That's it, lady? Your little classmate got hurt feelings?" He closes his eyes, facing forward again. "You're wasting our time with stupid stuff like this."

"Excuse me? *Stupid?* It's the principle—!"

"The *principle?*" Not bothering to look at her, Earwig waves away her witness. The *principle*, he mutters, intending to be heard, is that anti-Semites include "Jew-hating Jews" who bob their noses, change their names, turn their backs on their religion—

"Hey, wait a minute," Olin protests. "That's too easy."

"He knows nothing about me!" the woman wails, glaring around her for support. Further outraged when nobody speaks up, she sits down noisily, pops right back up to announce her refusal from now on to eat or even speak with "all these Germans. These people had no right to come! They should be ashamed!"

"We *are* ashamed, madame," Rainer says quietly. "Deeply ashamed. That is why we are here. We are scarred for life and coming here won't heal that."

Earwig points. "How about Ay-rabs, lady? We got one here from Palestine. You also refuse to eat with this nice Se-mite?"

The formidable Adina rises with an exasperated groan and a backhand flick of long ringed fingers that dismisses both antagonists and their whole disgraceful exchange. Ignoring Miriam as an unworthy foe, she confronts Earwig. "Yes, of course, Mr.—*Earwig*, is it?—the Arabs are a Semitic-*language* people, true. But isn't Jewish hatred inevitable when their leaders deny that the Shoah occurred and are sworn to drive every last Israeli Jew into the sea?"

And Miriam, not to be ignored, chimes in, "And anyway—come on, people, let's face it, okay? You've seen 'em yourself on the TV. They look like a *different* kind of a Semitic, right?"

"More swarthy, perhaps?" A new voice with a soft British inflection.

In the back row, the young Palestinian, long black hair tied up in a ponytail, has already risen; he is suddenly noticed, standing quiet a few moments in a room full of uneasy shifting. "Good evening," he murmurs politely. "Greetings from Palestine."

"Raghead! Better you should just shut up!" an American-born Israeli hollers, though begged by his wife to sit down and be quiet.

"You call them raghead, yes?" the young man continues. "Call them coward terrorist, these brave young fools with no future and no hope in life, gone crazy in the desert . . ." Here a deft pause for a twitched smile. Slowly, then, within his well-wrought isolation, he resumes his seat.

Olin exchanges a wry wince with Anders: so much for ecumenical healing and world peace.

"A pity our eloquent Muslim friend cannot speak for all his people." Adina's stiff smile tests the silence in the hall. "'In God We Trust,' you Americans say, but this man's Allah—or our Hebrew Yahweh, for that matter—serves the purpose just as well." Monotheism by whatever name has been the rationale for war and genocide forever. And the Unchosen, the inferior Others, are always demonized as an excuse to oppress them, isn't that true? And with God's blessing. "Thus"—and her accusing glance sweeps quickly past the Germans—"*Gott mit uns.*"

"*Gott mit uns!*" Anders whispers hoarsely. "If *Gott* vas *mit* those Nazi *Schweinehunde*, why didn't '*uns*' win the war?"

"*Nein!*" Seeing them grin, a German woman protests, "*Gott* iss not for funny business in *der Lager!*"

"*Gott* iss not for wisecrackers!" Rainer observes, trying not to laugh.

("I never thought Germans had much humor," Anders comments. "The men guffaw loud enough to crack your ears but there's no real mirth behind it—" He is checked by his roommate's grin. "What's so funny, Olin?"

"Sorry, but there are exceptions." He recalls a gravestone epitaph he'd seen one day in a cemetery in Berlin. *Fifty years I have perfect health. Now this!* And Anders hoots, "Sounds more like a Jew to me.")

At the intermission, Adina laments the fading interest in the Shoah among young people in Israel, where any mention of it may be met these days with bored indifference: it is stale history, the new generations say, as wearisome as those dreary old survivors and their nightmares. Even worse, say too many young Israelis, most of those survivors had been sluts or cowards.

"*What?* Snot-nose bastards. What do *they* know about it?"

"Bravo! Yes! Correct!" A young Zionist kibbutznik, full of himself to bursting: "So who's not sick of all this shit about the Shoah, right? Okay? So never again no more kvetching, okay? The survivors say, 'Forgive the unforgivable,' okay? So we forgive those people." He points rudely at the Germans. "Let them sit in their old Nazi shit for a thousand years, okay? But in Israel we are home and we are staying, and all those Arabs can go fuck themselves while we move on."

If that kid has moved on, Olin is thinking, why is he so angry? Why has he spent good money on this pilgrimage into the past which by the looks of him he can't afford? He shakes off Anders, who is chuckling into his ear again: "So now we move on, we go ethnic-clean, okay? Croats, maybe? Those Croats might be very nice today."

"Some of us can never move on," intones the melancholy Rabbi Glock, who for a thin man has too much tremble in his chin. And Earwig snarls to no one in particular, "You sucked it up in your mother's milk, that hate." Which hate? Olin wonders. For all the sincere good will, there are so many old hates in this hall. Earwig, for instance—who does this guy hate most? Nazis? Catholics? Georgie Earwig? The human species? Who had his mother been, and where?

Swooping in to tidy up her point, the Israeli professor wishes to register her solidarity with the young kibbutzniks. (Being young at heart herself, is what she means, says Anders.) Yes, it is time to move on. All those wars and massacres, those genocides, those hordes of refugees walking endless dust-choked roads to nowhere, scouring the earth for the last food and water—aren't these never-ending tragedies of our own time dreadful enough without clinging to the Catastrophe of fifty years ago?

Dr. Anders Stern, setting levity aside, interrupts his esteemed colleague to protest. The Shoah was different from anything before it, a realm of horror so far exceeding past insanities as to risk escaping human history altogether. In the end, he says, all this race business is meaningless. "*Jewish* blood? What is it, really?"

The American Israeli is up again. "After so much, he wants to know what's Jewish blood?"

Professor Schreier raises hand and voice. "Understand, Dr. Stern, I don't mean to exempt Israel from criticism. To judge from our record in Palestine, we have learned very little from our own great tragedy. It's all very well to observe Holocaust Day and blow that siren; I myself have cried, '*Never again!*' on the street corner in Tel Aviv—"

The American Israeli: "So what side are you on, lady? You a *real* Israeli or just some kind of a jihadnik—?"

"Hey, let her finish!" calls another man. "Look where we find ourselves these days with our homegrown apartheid!"

Adina nods and frowns at the same time. "That apartheid analogy is anti-Semitism, too, of course. True, our leaders invite it—"

"Right on, Prof!" bawls Earwig. "And when your bullet-headed politicians run out of cheap tricks and your swarthy inferiors are still standing in your way, what happens then? The Final Solution to the *Ay*-rab Question?"

The audience turns on him in a body, pointing fingers at his face. *Who is this guy anyway?* Another voice: *All you damned Jews in the Diaspora—!* Earwig cringes comically in this wave of denunciation, even summons it with the cupped fingers of both outstretched hands, as in *Bring it on, you sons-of-bitches, let's see what you got.*

"Diaspora, my ass-pora," he jeers. And it is now, in the ensuing uproar, that he turns and enlists Olin with a burlesqued wink of complicity.

Why you dirty bastard! To compromise someone else so casually—how infuriating! Olin summons up a sort of smile intended to suggest that this guy's outrages are mere childish provocations, not to be taken seriously. But Earwig won't help even a little by returning Olin's smile, for Earwig smiles rarely and never laughs, not ever, despite his chronic air of bitter amusement. The man is dead honest, Olin reminds himself, and he has honor of a kind and no self-pity: he does not hint at some horrific past to excuse his nastiness. But that gullied face, those ravines flanking his nose: Is this attrition what Ben Lama wishes everyone to see? That "G. Earwig, unaffiliated," hunkered in his seat, could use a little healing, too? Does anyone have any idea where this man comes from, or care?

Anders is still holding forth as they get ready for bed. As an evolutionary biologist, he questions whether a potential for evil behavior can be called "unnatural" or "inhuman": if it is latent in our nature, as he believes, it is all too human. Our closest relative, the chimpanzee, can be brutal, murderous, but it is never evil, intentionally doing harm. A male lion may bloodily devour its young. But *Homo sapiens* is the only animal that will knowingly torment others, the weaker individuals of its own species perhaps especially. Thus the depraved Nazi trooper is lower than the beast because the beast knows nothing of the joys of cruelty—

"So the death camp is no aberration, only an extreme sociopathic manifestation of man's fundamental nature, is that your point? I understand this, Anders, so if you don't mind, I'm turning off the light."

UNABLE TO SLEEP, he rises, dresses, makes his way downstairs and out into the streets, circling the *Lager*'s outer walls to the liver-colored bourgeois house at 88 Legion Street, just outside the barbed wire on the camp corner—the former habitation of camp Commandant Rudolf Franz Ferdinand Hoess, with its military row of hard tight evergreens and its concrete dog pen of a garden and its view down the perimeter street to the artificial pine knoll camouflaging the munitions bunker that served as the camp's first gas chamber and crematorium.

Rudolf Hoess has mainly interested Olin because before his execution he composed a memoir said to be mostly trustworthy. At the end of World War I, age seventeen, he served as the youngest noncommissioned officer in the German army. Joining Hitler's party in 1922, he soon proved his mettle by committing a political murder for its leaders and enduring six years in prison. In 1934, Hoess was conscripted for the black-booted SS; in official photographs of its high-ranking officers, he is the stocky man seen often at the elbow of his mentor, Minister of the Interior Heinrich Himmler, the tall triple-chinned Minister of the Interior in bottle-bottomed glasses. In May of 1940, after a tour of duty at the Sachsenhausen camp, Hoess was transferred to Oswiecim, bringing with him a squad of thirty condemned criminals to carry out SS orders as the barracks *Kapos*. By his own account, Hoess took such pride in his efficiency that photographers were invited from Berlin to record his operation for unlucky colleagues who had had no opportunity to visit.

Like perpetrators of atrocities worldwide, Rudolf Hoess would lay all blame on his superiors, describing himself as "a normal person overcome by a ruthless concept of obedience." This appraisal of his own character seems almost rational when compared to the vainglory of Adolf Eichmann, for whom the knowledge that he helped consign five million Jewish human beings to their deaths was a source of "extraordinary satisfaction." "I shall leap into my grave laughing," Eichmann said.

The house is silent, its windows dead, yet in some dimension it is still inhabited, Olin thinks, by fat old Widow Hoess. "My family, to be sure, were well-provided for here in Auschwitz," Hoess would write. "Every wish expressed by my wife or children was granted them. The children could live a free and untrammeled life. My wife's garden was a paradise of flowers."

The Hoesses and their four offspring, waited on by emaciated slaves, inhabited a brute heaven of gourmet delicacies, silks, furs, jewelry, and assorted loot stripped from doomed prisoners. His wife would sigh, "I want to live here till I die," according to one slave (who may have survived, Olin supposes, thanks to furtive access to the family's garbage). But Frau Hoess's gourmandizing rapture, uninhibited by her surroundings, was matched by the indifference to human suffering not only of her husband and the SS and the *Kapos* in the camp but of those local people who took jobs inside these gates.

A surge of hatred: he is suddenly out of breath. ("They grew fond of certain slaves, we've heard," red-haired Rebecca, his friend from Warsaw, has told him, "but as good Germans, they let them be taken to the ovens when their turn came.")

After the war, the fugitive Hoess worked on a German farm until his arrest; like Hans Frank, the Nazi governor in Cracow who made off with the Leonardo, he was found guilty at Nuremberg of crimes against humanity, returned to Poland, and condemned to death. In April 1947, the last breath was yanked from stocky stone-faced SS Obersturmbannführer Rudolf Hoess on gallows erected near the entrance of his Krematorium #1.

SIX

Separate prayer services for Buddhists, Jews, and Christians will be held each day on the platform or at the crematoria, and this morning, Olin accompanies the Israeli professor to the Christian service, which is led not by Father Mikal, who stands apart, but by Sister Catherine in the blue beret. Though Adina mostly agrees with Earwig's anti-clerical opinions, she deplores his abuse of the young women as inimical to the spirit of the retreat. Furthermore, she has formed a good opinion of the older novice, whom she has sought out and spoken with.

He listens dutifully to Sister Catherine, bows his head during the prayer, and under his breath joins in the simple hymn caroled by the novices as they lead their little congregation back toward the circle. The pure voices rising and falling on a cold east wind out of Ukraine seem to him beautiful.

During meditation, breathing mindfully moment after moment, his awareness opens and dissolves into snow light. But out of nowhere, just as he had feared, the platform's emptiness is filled by a multitude of faceless shapes milling close around him. He feels the vibration of their footfalls.

AT NOON EACH DAY outside the Gate, a wagon dispenses chunks of dark bread and a plain broth: the symbolic meal is eaten standing, using mouth and fingers in memory of those whose daily ration was foul watery gruel with a hunk of moldy crust.

In the shadow of the Arch, Sister Catherine dips her bread, neat as a squirrel. When he approaches to thank her for her morning service, she says, "All are welcome, sir." The other novice gawks at him with peasant frown. "Here is Sister Ann-Marie," says Sister Catherine, as if presenting a dull child, and her companion, closing her mouth, performs a clumsy sort of curtsy. Sister Ann-Marie is a short, heavy girl of thick complexion who, Olin suspects, has had less difficulty than she might have wished obeying her vow of chastity and probably has always known that she exists to serve. To judge from the sullen look of her, this does not mean she understands why this should be so, far less why she should accept her ordained lot without complaint.

When Sister Catherine attempts to thank him for intervening at the Kolbe chapel, he assures her he had meant only to protest that loud bullying of defenseless young women—here he stops short, for she is trying not to smile.

Is it because of his own prejudice that nuns make him so nervous? "You are Sister Katarzyna," he says in Polish. "And your maiden name?" She closes her eyes for a moment before watching him turn red. *Who would ask such a fool question?* In English, she says, "I am called Sister Catherine."

From the start, Sister Ann-Marie, with little English and no apparent interest in acquiring more, seems excluded from their conversation, though she stands right there. This bothers him more than it seems to bother Sister Catherine, who has scarcely glanced at the other woman since introducing her.

Sister Catherine has noticed after all that he's been taking notes, for she holds up her own diary. "You see? Nuns bear witness, too." When he confesses he has not come here to bear witness, she shrugs this off, not interested. "Doctor Professor D. Clements Olin, Polish-borned teacher-poet, yes? Who disapprove our Roman Church?" She waves the small green book at his eyes as if it contained proof.

"Not at all," he lies, taken aback. "I attended your service this morning—"

The second novice suddenly exclaims, "You speak our tongue!"—accusingly, as if he were trying to conceal this fact for nefarious reasons. "Well, yes, Sister," he says, holding Sister Catherine's eye. "At least I used to." And Sister Catherine, gazing straight into his face, says, "Sir, your spirit is hostile. Like your friend."

"He's not—" But he stops right there. To repudiate Earwig at this point would be weakness, perhaps some sort of betrayal, though in this moment he cannot think why.

Inspecting the bottom of her bowl, Sister Catherine is frowning now and blushing, too, apparently discomfited by her own bluntness. She is taller and older than the other, probably in her early thirties and similarly dressed in an ill-cut black cape and brown wool suit and galoshes. Her expression is quick and in its way fresh and appealing. Bright hazel eyes, uneven teeth, round red cheeks chafed—her skin looks sort of *scraped*. Gray-brown lips, plump but unpainted—a pity, he thinks, that she knows nothing of cosmetics. She doesn't really need to look so plain.

He wants very much to be straightforward; her candor demands no less. "It's only all that antiquated dogma—"

Sister Catherine actually steps backward as if slapped hard in the face. Sensing trouble from this foreigner, this *male*, her sister groans. "Yes," frowns Sister Catherine after a moment, "yes, there is much to understand." She taps her diary. "So far not much," she admits. That small pained smile comes and goes.

On impulse, she thrusts the journal into his hands. "In here I practice my bad English," she says. "Nothing is hiding." Startled by such recklessness, he hastens to explain that while he is interested, of course, in a nun's impressions—

"And you?" She points at his own notebook. "What is it? You reveal dark secret of Jew persecution by Saint Maximilian?" Her voice is soft but her face is tight.

To avoid any obligation to exchange notes, he tries again to return the diary, at the same time smiling to assure her that this fraught moment need not come between them, but she, perverse, won't extend her hand to take it. "So. Dr. Clements, Dr. Olin, no need for nice nun witness after all?" More irony. Challenged, he opens the diary to this morning's entry.

Just as he feared, she has discovered that the atmosphere in Birkenau is still swarming with "lost souls." Oh Lord, he thinks, all those poor wandering souls! Many retreatants, he suspects, share her belief that the unburied dead—"the hungry ghosts," as Ben Lama's Buddhists call them—still haunt this emptiness, unable to find rest because they were forsaken. The more devotional go further, seeking to console through prayer the keening spirits that their mission has stirred up like a wind of bees. How fatuous, he thinks.

Those multitudes are gone forever into a disappearing past beyond all healing, leaving no trace more tangible than the near-dust of all that hair in the museum.

She watches intently as he reads. And he is intrigued, despite himself, because she, too, has already been swarmed by those imaginary multitudes.

"Those feet passed right in front of me," he whispers. "Some in ripped shoes, as you say, but many naked!"

But she seems uninterested in any bond their visions of naked feet might create between them. Her expression says, *Never mind those feet, get on with it.*

Her hazel eyes search his face until he finishes. It's those brows that curve down around the eyes that bring a wistful cast to her expression, a shadow of sadness, he decides. He extends the diary again, nodding judiciously. "Well said, Sister Catherine. Rather beautiful, I think." Braving that gaze, he insists, "And please believe me, Sister, I do not feel hostile. I'm just troubled by the whole idea of papal infallibility—"

She snatches back her notebook, sets his empty bowl in hers, and returns both to the tailgate of the food truck on her way to the tunnel, Sister Ann-Marie stumping behind. Not until she nears the meditation circle on the platform does she turn to face him. She takes a deep breath. "Sir, His Holiness . . ." She is unable to finish.

At the circle bundled figures turn toward the burr of

their low voices. He must clear things up quickly, put this
bad start behind them.

᠊ᢘᢘ᠊

BY MIDAFTERNOON soft snow is falling, muffling four
voices that rise from the cardinal points around the circle,
north, south, east, and west, intoning names from registration lists obtained by Rainer from museum archives in
Berlin—long lists that represent but tiny fractions of that
fraction of new prisoners who survived, however briefly,
the first selections on this platform and were tattooed with
small blue numbers. The impeccable lists include city and
country of origin, arrival date, and date of death, not infrequently on that same day or the next.

Column after column, page after page, of the more
common family names ascend softly from the circle of still
figures to be borne away on gusts of wind-whirled snow.
*Schwartz, Herschel; Schwartz, Isaac A.; Schwartz, Isaac D.;
Schwartz, Isidor— Who? Isidor? You too?* The voices are
all but inaudible as befits snuffed-out identities that exist
only on lists, with no more reality than forgotten faces in
old photo albums—*Who's this bald guy in the back?* Stray
faces of no more significance than wind fragments of these
names of long ago, of no more substance than this snow-

flake poised one moment on his pen before dissolving into voids beyond all knowing.

※

MENTION OF NAME-CHANTING that evening sends one German, Horst, off on another rant. To speak seriously of murder facilities with impeccable registration lists is utterly insane, the man is yelling, because death camps themselves are beyond all sane discussion, even by those few who survived. So how could mere visitors hope to grasp something unrecognizable even as pathology to anybody who is not insane himself?

Ben Lama nods. "There's no space left on that platform for interpretation. It's just there," he says. "It just *is*."

※

TOWARD TWILIGHT, the sharp-winged silhouette of a small falcon crosses the no-man's-land of charred black chimneys—the only wild thing he has seen besides rooks in raucous flight over the snow-patched fields between the great dead camp and the world out there on the horizon, no farther from the platform than those faint church bells, that far rumbling of trains.

Olin? You're right here in the region. Why do you wait?
He must at least try to locate some old inhabitant with a
dim memory of the burned manor house or even, possibly,
a clue as to the fate of that other family. He will go make
inquiries, of course. Perhaps tomorrow.

⁜

AS A LANDED ARISTOCRAT, ill-read and a bit obtuse, the
Anglophile old Baron in his cuff-scuffed suits from Jermyn
Street, his Lock hat and Lobb shoes from St. James's, had
been by his own comfortable description "a damned unre-
pentant snob." His son Alexei had inherited his father's
prejudice against "the Romans," which was not only permissible, damn it all, but a prerogative of one's legacy and
common sense, and as a consequence of anti-clerical family
attitudes, Clements worried that he himself might be a re-
flexive anti-papist. However, what worried him far more
was how careless bias against Roman Catholics was used to
paint over the mold and rot of a far more pernicious prejudice against the Jews.

Olin's Lutheran grandparents and their émigré friends
had no hesitation in blaming Rome-stoked hatred for the
demonizing of the Jews; for a thousand years, thanks to
the clergy, anti-Semitism had been as ingrained in the
coarse hides of Polish "serfs" as the earth under their fin-

gernails, the old Baron said. Why else would so many uned-
ucated Poles—and Croats, Ukrainians, Romanians, and
other Catholics—have done so much of the dirty work for
the Gestapo and the SS and, farther east, for the Soviet secret police?

Though escape abroad had spared them harsh experience of either, the family had of course abhorred the loutish
Nazis, then the barbaric Red soldiery who despoiled their
chalet and estate. Appalled by that upstart in Berlin ("He
brings his mouth to his food, they say, instead of his food
to his mouth") they professed great sympathy—*mais oui!*—
for those unfortunate "Israelite" victims. (Was "Jew" a
dirty word?) But the old Baron's sniffing enunciation, his
sifting of such words like small bones in the fish course,
instantly (and to some degree intentionally, his grandson
suspected) laid bare that time-honored disdain—not quite
overt, always deniable, yet as pervasive in that house as the
faint reek of Alexei's old retriever.

Growing up and learning more, Clements came to recognize the racist slights that surfaced in dinner conversations, those casual unkindnesses, occasionally quite clever
(and considered more permissible on that account), that
soiled his sense of self-respect when he smiled, too. The
meanness was in the timing, the inflection. And in his
youth, he'd often wondered what awful secret about Jews
these émigré aristocrats seemed to know, when as a class,

he was discovering, they knew so little of real substance about *anything*.

The boy supposed he loved his family, what was left of it, since that, said his English grandmother, is "what one did." But eventually he realized that in this household, the Shoah had never been experienced as an immense tragedy involving unthinkable numbers of fellow Europeans, but only as an abstract calamity, as far removed from real concern as mention of some overcrowded ferry lost in the eastern seas. And as time went on, he came to understand that he himself had been unseen in the same way.

IN THE COLD MESS HALL, the evening meal is somber. Olin eats in silence with Anders and Rainer, the intense retreat leader from Berlin, and Eva, a Czech whose mother had survived the first selection only to die within the next few hours (of heartbreak, says her daughter). With Eva is another elderly survivor who smiles gently when spoken to but rarely speaks; he takes no notice when Eva whispers, "Mr. Malan is a great, great artist."

Sounding tired and discouraged, the old lady comments that to judge from the rude impatience of the few young people on this retreat, the Shoah has already lost its power as a cautionary lesson. Olin agrees. In reactionary circles in America, he tells them, despite the massive documentation, its very historical existence has been questioned, and even the degree of German guilt. He cites a right-wing Catholic review that bitched in print after the war about America's "over-exposure to the luridities . . . the countless corpses and gas ovens, and kilos of gold wrenched out of dead men's teeth. There is underway a studious attempt to cast suspicion upon Germany . . ."

"*Cast suspicion?*" Rainer yelps. "What nonsense! My country of Germany was guilty! Guilty, guilty, guilty! We admit this freely! Our own historians were already documenting every horrible detail in the very first days after the war! *A thousand years will pass and still Germany's guilt will not have been erased.* Hans Frank, the head Nazi in Cracow, wrote that in his death cell memoir!"

(Borowski said it better, Olin thinks: *In German cities the store windows are filled with books and religious objects but the smoke from the crematoria still hovers above the forests.*)

"Well, that's *something* to our credit, at least," sighs a German woman sitting nearby. Already offended by Earwig at her own table, she is taking refuge in their conversation.

"Bullshit." Earwig's voice is low and hard. "Give credit? To Kraut butchers mopping up the blood after they finish? Postwar Germany is crawling with old Nazis and fucking skinheads. Does this *Hausfrau*"—he points his full fork at her face—"honestly believe that under the covers it's any less anti-Semitic than it was before?"

"*Ja, ja!* I don't only belief it, sir, I *know* it—!"

"Or Poland? Or anywhere in Europe?" He turns back to his food. "In your dreams, Fräulein."

There's no bottom to this sonofabitch, Olin thinks. But rather than provoke another scene, he turns his back on Earwig with a loud scrape of his chair and changes the subject. What sort of Shoah education is received these days by Polish youth? he asks the table: he is thinking of Wanda and Mirek. All unhappily agree with Earwig that anti-Semitism, deep in the European grain, is probably ineradicable. "Polish kids made dreadful signs to passing cattle cars," Eva recalls, drawing a weak finger across her throat. Anders says that his fellow Swedes, despite their bland and neutral reputation, are just as prejudiced as all the rest. He doubts that bringing schoolchildren here on field trips as a cautionary lesson would accomplish much.

"Besides giving 'em some good ideas for next time, maybe," Earwig calls, the words dripping from his tongue like cold drops from the tip of a dirty icicle.

Anders brays and others snicker and the coven of Warsaw intelligentsia looks sardonically amused to hear the youth of Poland being jeered at. And Olin, amused, too, but determined not to show it, wonders aloud if even in this camp's darkest days—or in those darkest days perhaps especially—there weren't little eruptions of black humor.

"In the extermination camps? Never," old Eva whispers with a palsied shaking of the balding skull of airy white hair that perches atop her spine like a worn-out duster. "Not ever. Never." She cannot recall seeing an inmate smile in all her long years in the camps, not even the *Kapos*: that expression those brutes wore, she moans, could never be mistaken for a smile. And she recalled once more how *Kapos* greeted the new prisoners by pointing at the smoke: "The only way you will ever leave this place is up those chimneys"—that was *Kapo* humor. Poor Eva is so shaken that when Olin apologizes for being insensitive, she chooses not to hear him, and when the conversation turns in a new direction, the old woman falls aside in a kind of trance.

Dr. Anders Stern commandeers a stilted silence, warming instantly to his own favorite subject. Auschwitz-Birkenau, he pontificates, is all the proof needed that as a species, the human animal has never lost the most primitive traits of the primate predator-scavenger on the savanna, the incipient killer. Morally, man's consciousness has made no progress in all the millennia since his graffiti first defaced cave walls. "We regress, in fact," he says, as Adina Schreier, attracted by any opportunity to debate her fellow academic, draws up a chair. "Our man-ape ancestors, being merely animal," he is saying, "were surely less sadistic than the *Homo* species we call '*sapiens*'—"

"Yes, yes, of course, but these are scarcely new ideas,"

the professor says. "'Our much-praised technological progress, and civilization generally, could be compared to an
axe in the hand of a pathological criminal.' That's Einstein,
in a letter to a friend while still in Germany. He already
understood these things in the early thirties."

Anders looks cross because Adina has derailed his dis-
quisition just as it was gathering steam, and Adina is cross
because Ben Lama had not consulted anyone before giving
permission to a small film crew to come document his pioneer retreat. ("No starring role for the famous Israeli professor, that's what annoys her," Anders advises Olin in a
stage whisper, loud as usual.)

"Is it really so simple?" Olin asks, impatient with them
both. "Incipient evil in human nature? Technological progress versus pathological axe murders? Why can't I take that
on faith, even from Einstein?"

"Nor I, sir! I don't believe that either!" protests Eva.
"There were kind acts also—*extraordinary* acts!"

The ironical Swede marvels aloud that this old woman
sentenced to death for partisan activities had survived five
years in a Slovenian camp.

"What are you suggesting, sir?" Her frail voice rises.
"I fought hard to save my soul! I fought hard, yes," she
whispers as tears come. "And yes—if this is what you
wish to hear, sir—yes, I was defeated. My very soul, it was
defeated."

Triumphant, Anders grins at Olin, who awards him a cold stare in return.

Adina Schreier, patting the old woman's hand, is glaring at the Swede: "You are happy now, sir? Shame on you!" But there it is, the fatal question, like an arched scorpion taut on the doorsill. *Five years, you say? Not so fast, madame. Pray tell us, how did you manage to survive so long? And at what cost to others?*

SEVEN

After supper, people gather slowly in the auditorium. On this second evening, most look stunned by Birkenau, and the mood is darkening. The German woman who rejoiced the day before in the forgiving spirit of the gathering complains tonight that she is barely tolerated here as "just another guilty German": never before has she felt the burden of her nationality in this painful way.

"It's about time, then!" taunts She Who Won't Eat with Germans.

"So maybe yes, it is 'about time,' so maybe you are correct, madam." The German woman concurs earnestly but perseveres. "Still, it is hurting very much. Today the singing of our hymns is weak because few come to join our Christian service. Today even, I see some turn their backs. We Christians seem to be in the wrong place here."

"*We Germans*, you mean."

"*Nein! Nein!* She does *not* mean!" Rainer jumps up to defend her. "Many Germans—nowhere near as many as now claim it but maybe more than our Jewish comrades here may think—they hated the Nazis, too."

"Only because of your lost war and your bombed-out cities and the piles of your own dead and no damned food—you Germans love to eat," calls Earwig. "Nothing to do with murdered Jews."

But the audience has had enough of Earwig, and some who have only muttered now speak out: Who *is* that guy? What's he doing here? someone complains. Another: Is he with us or against us, for Christ's sake? And a third voice, louder: Hey, Ben? Come on, man! Throw him out!

Before we lynch him? Olin thinks. *Is that already in the air?*

Ben Lama slips into one of the seats beside Earwig, which are always empty. He does not remonstrate or even speak; the action itself subdues the man. Almost alone among the Jews, Ben seems untroubled by that lacerating tongue; in fact, he has already told Olin how much he appreciates this guy's remarks, which cut away the devotional hushed speech and pseudo-spiritual manner that afflict too many participants, getting in the way of true empathy and clarity. "I agree, he's pretty rough. But have you heard him say anything untrue?" Yesterday Olin saw Ben quake with silent mirth when Earwig, in a mock response to a reproof from a Zen monk, stared in alarm at the monk's shaved pate, then pushed his palms upward just above his ears like a woman adjusting her hat. "Please, sir," he whined, "would you mind fluffing that up a little?"

In the bad silence, Ben Lama tells the audience a story about Master Joshu and his monk, who come to a clearing in the forest only to see all the animals run away. "Why do they flee?" cries the monk. "Don't they know you are a great Zen master?" And Joshu smiles. "Perhaps. But they also know I am a killer." And Ben smiles, too.

Earwig surprises Olin with the lack of edge in his attitude toward the teacher. "This Ben guy," he says later. "I thought he was soft but he's really pretty tough. No mushy feel-good New Age jargon, stays real cool about other people's bullshit. 'I see,' he says. And what does he see? He sees what a stupid asshole you can be but leaves you space to see that for yourself."

"So you see it for yourself now, right?"

There it is, the chink: what flickers across his face is less grin than grimace. He can welcome public denunciation, but hard teasing is another matter. Olin regrets having made fun of him, but not much; the man's own teasing is never well-meant or constructive, it is merely hard.

OLIN HAPPENED to be watching Sister Catherine when she was approached before the meeting by a man arrived earlier that day—"a defrocked monk," according to Adina. When the man attempted to draw her aside, she stiffened, wouldn't be led: the two stood at odds, too far apart, in a sort of wary sideways confrontation. She was expressionless, gaze cast down, and his forced smile was painful. They entered the auditorium and not together.

Before the testimonies can resume, Sister Catherine rises. She wishes to thank Jewish and German friends who have attended Christian service on the platform at Birkenau and to welcome any who might wish to join them in coming days.

Looking discomfited, Priest Mikal shifts in his seat. If the priest feels the novice is out of order, as he seems to, why hasn't he welcomed all these Jews himself?

The auditorium is still grumbling and restless. Voices rise in complaint and chairs are barged around more noisily than necessary, until finally Rainer bounds onto the stage, shouting harshly for order. Apparently Rainer has been chided about his forceful Kaddish at the Black Wall that first morning, because hearing the resonance of his own shout in the startled room, he shakes his head in disbelief at its officiousness and apologizes sheepishly for "being so Cher-man." Olin realizes he likes this man very much.

Relating his experience as a boy in wartime Munich, Rainer describes how his gentle Uncle Werner, in the naive hope he might protect her, confessed his love for a Jewish girl to the authorities; not only did he fail to save her, but found himself immediately conscripted and cynically assigned to the SS here in Auschwitz, where he was bullied, beaten, and eventually castrated for refusing to carry out some sadistic command.

"I am here to honor him," Rainer says. Until his death many years after the war, his uncle remained an outcast in the family. "Why? Because in their hearts they had never forgiven him for disgracing the family with his love for a Jew." Rainer coughs, fighting down his grief all these years later for "that brave good man," who long after the war was scarcely permitted to slink along the edges of family occasions.

In his distress, Rainer has reverted to that big voice of his. Like so many Germans, he shouts, his family contracted the disease of that sick fascism in which what formerly would have been condemned as unspeakable cruelty was extolled as patriotic duty. Worse, they clung to their delusion even after three million of their own soldiers and civilians were destroyed. Worse still, he says, that mortality was widely seen in Germany as more than sufficient compensation for the Third Reich's share of the estimated fourteen

million Europeans, most of them Jews, who had been murdered by Germany and Russia. "Can you believe this?" he
asks bitterly. "They were actually sorry for themselves."

EAGER TO DECLARE their nation's shame before others
can imply it, the Germans have been far more forthcoming
than the Poles, including the group of Warsaw intelligentsia who have adopted Clements Olin.

At the edge of this group, never quite included, is Stefan, the man Olin has observed trying to speak with Sister
Catherine; a former monk, Stefan had trained in the same
seminary as Priest Mikal. Stefan's priory is in the region of
the notorious Treblinka death camp north of Warsaw, by
repute even more terrible than Birkenau; nobody, he says,
ever escaped Treblinka and survived. He claims this with
an air of perverse pride as if vaunting his district soccer
team. He also seems proud of his excommunication from
the Church for submitting a reform petition to the new Polish pope without seeking approval from the bishop, knowing that any such attempt to circumvent the hierarchy
would be useless. In a symbolic but futile gesture, he says,
he finally knelt before the altar and stripped off his rope
belt and brown cassock.

The Polish group has also adopted Eva's friend, the artist Malan, a self-taught painter who survived four years in this camp, then returned from Warsaw in old age to create a huge fresco on the cellar walls of a closed chapel within distant sight of the high tower at Birkenau. Malan has invited Olin to come inspect his work-in-progress, which Eva calls extraordinary, and Olin has promised he will visit there in the next days.

The first Pole to go forward is his friend Rebecca, who clomps onto the stage and promptly offends some in her audience with her reminder that Auschwitz had dealt mostly with the Jews of western Europe, and that by the time the death factory at Birkenau became operational in the winter of 1942, a far more extensive genocide had already decimated the so-called *Ostjude* of eastern Poland, the Baltics, Byelorussia, and Ukraine. Before the war, Becca's home city of Warsaw had the largest Jewish community on earth, she says, but few of its Jews wound up in Auschwitz: more than a million, transported eastward, died in smaller, more primitive "facilities" such as Treblinka.

"Correct," quavers a long-bearded old man who as a boy had witnessed from hiding the bloody murder of his family in Ukraine's Babi Yar ravine. Most of those Jews in the East were never arrested or imprisoned, he says, simply rounded up with the aid of local Slavs and confined in open pens without shelter, food, or water until they died; others were asphyxiated by exhaust fumes piped into the backs of idling vans and trucks. But most were marched into the forests, where the SS made do with bullets in the back of the head as they knelt in prayer at the edge of enormous pits dug by themselves. That so few survivor accounts emerged from the ruins of eastern Europe was partly because so few literate victims survived to testify, and also because the new satellite states stifled all reports of Russian participation in atrocities. In the histories, the wretched millions killed from Warsaw eastward became little more than a chapter note in the great modern tragedy of the Jewish people.

ONSTAGE, BECCA is lamenting an irrepressible young cousin whose father had constructed a secret hiding place in his Warsaw house. As the Gestapo broke their door down with violent shouts and banging, the terrified little girl wailed in the dark and could not be hushed. Rather than suffocate his favorite child, she said, the father led his family out of hiding, pleading for mercy. All would die at Auschwitz but that little girl crouched unnoticed in the hiding place, an irony that the child herself, as the agent of her family's end, would mourn forever.

Her friend Nadia's wince confirms Olin's suspicion that the noisy child had been Rebecca, who in her warm, abundant way remains unstifled to this day.

The Polish men, arms folded on their chests, continue to

maintain a weary silence. Their recalcitrance is leaving the impression in the hall, as Becca warns them, that those damned Poles, unlike the Germans, have never faced up to their past and therefore have learned nothing for the future.

The men grin uncomfortably, indulging her, but none go to the podium. Knowing how harshly their country's collaboration has been condemned in the West, they seem to fear that any witness they might offer would be instantly dismissed as disingenuous or self-serving, probably both, and that the Jewish majority in this hall would only jeer them. When a voice calls out, "Time for you Poles to speak up!" Zygmunt, a sculptor, shouts back, "Unlike you, we Poles have learned to keep our mouths shut!"

"And yet you came," Olin reminds them quietly, inviting an explanation. The men shrug. Plainly they don't feel answerable to this pseudo-Pole, this damned American academic. Aggressively defensive, Zygmunt grumbles that they are here only as Zen practitioners, to lend moral support to Ben Lama's "well-meaning" retreat. The ex-monk Stefan hints that he might be doing penance for the role played by "certain clergy" in his country, but when Ben Lama, noticing him whispering, invites him to come forward so that everyone can benefit from his witness, Stefan points at Earwig instead. "Ask this man here. This man is very disagreeable, he is maybe a big liar, but he does not lie about the Vatican and Jews."

Jaroslav, Becca's companion, a violinist with long black

hair (that he probably slaps over his brow during perfor-
mances, decides Olin, who dislikes him), speaks so rarely
that first he must excavate his throat at unpleasant length.
"That Jew prayer at the Black Wall the first morning? For
the Dead? Why no mention of the Polish martyrs?" After
all, he says, it was mostly Poles who were executed at that
wall; the great majority of Jews came later and were taken
straight to Birkenau. "Today these Israelis fly their big blue
flag here, and Israel didn't even *exist* yet, for God's sake!"

"Why raise a flag at all? Who'd want to claim this
place?" Rebecca broods. "Sure, those Nazi pigs disgraced
themselves. They soiled themselves. Disgustingly." She
looks frankly at the Germans. "Yet in some way," she continues, "all those centuries of pogroms, then the Shoah—
hasn't all this suffering soiled the Jews, too?

"Who can we be as a people," she demands, "when century after century our fellow men despise us, cast us out?
What is so hateful about Jews that others need to demonize
and kill us? Bulldoze piles of our naked bodies into pits
like so much offal? What *is* this curse the so-called Chosen
People suffer? Can persecution be the fate that we were
chosen for? And if so, why? What did we do?"

She tosses her hands high—*"Aach!"*—to return that old
question to the rabbis. "These good kind Christians," she
tells Olin, indicating her friends, "rebuilt my city, all but—
can you guess?—the Jewish quarter! Is that because there
was nobody to put in it?"

"I AM FROM THE OTHER SIDE." Thrashing to her feet, a large raw-boned Polish woman with coarse hair tied back hard, baring her ears, speaks with defiance. The faces stare. *The other side?* What can that mean? Who is she? Why has she come? She does not say. She simply stands there, apparently on the point of another utterance, but when the cameraman turns his lens her way, she sits back down. Professor Schreier complains peevishly to Olin about losing their first local witness to that damned camera, which Adina sees as Ben Lama's hunger for publicity as well as an inexcusable intrusion. She intends to return to Israel on the very first flight out of Cracow day after tomorrow.

THE IDEA THAT A GENOCIDE far greater and more terrible had already occurred in eastern Europe has rankled many Jews from Europe and the United States, who are accustomed to having the Holocaust all to themselves. Anders parodies the sullen mutterings he pretends to have heard outside the hall: *"Filthy potato-eaters. Oy! Good riddance!"*

Olin smiles carefully, having learned long ago not to show too much amusement when Jews are being funny about Jews, not even when hilarious tales are told among his closest Jewish friends. Also, he wishes to be sure that his empathy with the people killed here is authentic, visceral, not merely an idea. As an American, he is embarrassed by loud Miriam, therefore a bit worried about the latent anti-Semitism in his own background: Would her crude manner be sufficient provocation, were he Jewish, to make him a genteel bigot like Kafka and Appelfeld and Bruno Schulz—all of them admirable Jewish writers whose cultured bourgeois families had been careful to avoid spas and public places infested by such people?

"Infested," Olin? You sure that's the word you want? Be very careful.

"Remember that movie about the young Polish mother on the platform who was ordered to choose between her two young kids?" Anders is saying. "We heard that your Jews in the U.S. complained that a Polish heroine had no business in an Auschwitz story, no, no, no! Auschwitz was a sacred shrine of the Jewish people."

Anders says he has always been embarrassed by Jews who insist that their suffering was more terrible than other people's. Sitting motionless on that platform all day long in winter weather, it has seemed to him more and more idle to judge whose ordeal had been worst. Or whose guilt, for that matter. Germans, Poles, Romanians, Croats, Ukrainians— are these ethnicities intrinsically more cruel, historically "worse" human beings than the racists and torturers in other lands? If so, does "worse" signify "inferior"? And if so, do these peoples remain inferior in perpetuity? Or should all *Homo sapiens* be given the benefit of the doubt by reason of incurable insanity? "Accept that we can't help ourselves, we're 'only human,'" Anders sneers, "and that even the most vicious Nazis started out as little children, sweet and innocent as you or me—"

"Born 'good Germans,' I suppose you mean," Olin agrees, "cute little tykes gradually corrupted through no fault of their own by state-mandated cruelties, first in small steps and then more fatally as greed took over, until the dread morning when those poor devils woke up as brand-new Nazis, right? In an evil world they never made—?"

Anders, laughing, wigwags both hands before his face to ward off all such sophistry. "Woke up in the wrong beer hall, is more like it!" he shouts gleefully.

UNABLE TO SLEEP, Olin lies unsmiling in the dark. He is thinking about his father. The onetime cavalry lieutenant's proud bearing had been sadly frayed by a loss of self-respect which on occasion would erupt in long-nursed grievance at his parents' failure to acknowledge his sacrifice in quitting his regiment on the eve of war to escort them in their flight from their homeland. Oh, how bitterly he had come to regret his deference to their appeals! Once they were safe, their gratitude was soon eroded by their disappointment in his subsequent behavior; they had simply chosen to forget how shamelessly they had coerced him, then denied him credit for the filial loyalty that was his sole excuse for betraying his soldier's honor. They'd even dared insinuate that Alexei had fled Poland out of cowardice, "abandoning our beloved homeland in its darkest hour," as the old Baron liked to phrase it, gazing east toward the Atlantic, in the general direction of Olinski honor.

AS A POSTWAR SCHOOLBOY, Clements had been fascinated by reports of the Nazi death camps—morbidly, according to his grandmother. Nobody at home so much as mentioned that the dread name in the news was only the German pronunciation of Oswiecim, the old provincial town near the family estate in Silesia. Nor was it revealed to him until years later that in the first months after his family's escape to America, word had come from the estate agent in Oswiecim that Clements's maternal grandmother, Emilie Adam, had been reported to the authorities as an "individual of Hebrew descent." Detained, then arrested, so the story went, she and her two daughters had been removed to the Cracow ghetto. In the stress of this emergency, her husband, Dr. Allgeier, had so strenuously objected that a kinswoman of the Count Potocki, a lady of the ancient Pilawa lineage, should be shouted at and pushed about like some shtetl dweller from Galicia, that he, too, was shouted at and pushed about, knocked down and shot.

In the boy's presence, this story was dismissed as vicious rumor and the estate agent denounced as an opportunist who had doubtless lied to the Gestapo in the honest hope of acquiring that fine house for himself. To all this, the boy listened and said nothing. But one of those Allgeier daughters, after all, had been his mother, and noting his peculiar expression, the old Baroness explained that the family had spared him this whole scurrilous story for fear it might upset him. Third- or fourth-hand rumors out of Occupied Poland could not be verified, of course, but neither could they be discounted out of hand.

In the end, the estate agent was paid much more than the family could afford to effect the abduction of the infant "David"—with the tearful cooperation of his mother, went the story—and his delivery into good hands at Gdansk for the ship voyage to London and the U.S.A., where he was speedily baptized in the Episcopal church and christened David Clements. Thenceforth and throughout his youth, the boy had been strictly discouraged from inquiring about his mother lest his curiosity upset "poor Alexei," who was so heartbroken by the disappearance of his great love in Poland that he wore a black armband in her memory year after year. And on many nights the boy was scared awake by a dream in which a mysterious young woman, whose face he had never seen even in photographs, had gone missing. His dread upon awakening, that she might have been exterminated, seemed so inevitable an explanation of her absence that the nightmare sickened him. Yet he never asked about her, not until years later, one afternoon at teatime when he was home from boarding school and his father was absent from the house. The Baroness dismissed his nightmare as some evil fume that had issued from some old rumor out of Poland. "It was in the air here, David. You might have picked up those morbid ideas of yours without quite knowing it."

That evening, his father, in his cups, related tearfully to his son how his noble Emi urged him to flee, he could send for her later if he wished, and so forth. The brave girl had insisted on staying behind, Alexei mourned, out of worry for her parents in the coming war and also lest they be deprived of the joy of their first grandchild. "*You*, my boy!"

"Father? Did you know before you left that she was pregant?"

"What's that? I'll thank you to speak more respectfully of your mother!"

His father vowed he would go find his Emi as soon as the Cold War was over and travel to Poland became possible, but when that time came, no effort was made by anybody in the family to determine the lost Emi's whereabouts ("if any," muttered the old lady). Instead, Alexei consoled himself by marrying his wealthy mistress, a "vulgar American as greedy for his title as he is for her money," said the Baroness. "She might even fit into his little red boots."

AFTER HIS MARRIAGE, Alexei almost retired the black armband. His new wife, however, approved the look of it, at least when worn with his dark worsteds in the winter and pale linen suits in summer. And of course he donned it dutifully again to honor one parent then the other at their funerals a few years later, the bitterly disappointed mother and the father who never liked him much and eventually shunted him out of the lineage in favor of the grandson Clements, now a graduate student at university.

Once the old people were gone, Alexei's Lily, apprised of Poland's multitudes of counts and barons, was able to persuade her "Sasha" to ignore his father's edict in regard to the baronetcy and award himself a higher rank while he was at it. ("Who gives a damn in America, my darling? I mean, there are so many of you!") A bit sheepish, the new Count Alexei assured his son that the landed aristocracy in old Poland would never have bothered their heads about such trifles.

Had his father been rather a silly fellow, Clements wondered? Sometimes it seemed so. But he must have been a very sad fellow as well, for not two years after the death of his parents, Count Alexei Olinski wandered out onto weak ice on the town pond in early spring, the canvas pockets of his hunting jacket stuffed with lead weights cut from the anchor lines of his old wood decoy ducks.

Putting on that armband for his father's funeral, Clements supposed that in wearing it, he was accepting a family responsibility for his mother, long neglected.

After the funeral, the Countess Lily had presented him with his grandfather's gold cuff links and also a stray photograph ("Yours now, I should think") that had turned up in his father's dresser drawer. In the creased snapshot, a laughing girl with wind-danced curls and a comical air leaned far out a thatched ground-floor window to hail a goose passing by along the street. How pretty she was! Could this black-haired girl have been his mother? And the photographer his father? They assumed so.

"Why did he never show this to me, then?"

"Nor to me. Nor to his parents, either, I shouldn't imagine." She contemplated the photo. "No, no, this girl belonged exclusively to Alexei, goose and all."

Really? he thought. Their son had no claim on her? But, stoic and reserved out of long habit, he kept these feelings to himself, where they belonged.

The sense of what she'd said overtook the Countess Lily a bit late. "Oh Christ," she complained, less cross with herself than with him. Her tone turned harsh and her manner coarse, for she was drunk. "Don't you ever complain, Clements? I mean, it can't be good for you, bottling things up the way you do. It's a little scary."

"Please, Lily. It's not important."

Deep in her armchair, steeped in whiskey, she considered her stepson, nodding as if to say, *Yes, this may hurt.* "Skipped out on all of us, even himself," she muttered. His stepmother was not unkind and nor was she quite bright, but she was straightforward and he trusted her. "Prettier than I ever was," she said, "and a lot more fun than *he* was, from the look of her."

She confessed she'd been jealous of Emi Allgeier before she understood how much Alexei had needed the disappearance of his great love in Poland, which affirmed the tragedy of war and loss that had given his life whatever resonance it had. She sometimes feared he'd only married his "American meal ticket" to avoid having to go abroad after the war to look for Emi and learn a painful truth he knew already, not that she was gone—surely the Olinskis had assumed that from the start?—but that she had been left behind through his weakness or betrayal or some failure of nerve that he could never face.

Had Alexei casually seduced and carelessly "knocked up" that little teacher, asked the Countess Lily, then snuck away to America without a word? And had he omitted this detail from his legend and lied about it ever since, first to his family and later to himself? "We might as well be honest, Clements. If I'm correct, the great love of his life became his lifelong shame. You never sensed this?

"No," she continued, seeing his expression, "I'm not imagining things, love." And out of guilt, her Alexei had let himself be bullied half to death by his dreadful parents. "And those old European snobs are *tough*! If I hadn't come along to rescue the poor guy and move him over here to my place, he might have died without ever leaving home."

As the last Olinski, Clements cropped that family name to "Olin," his school nickname all his life. With no ache of Poland in his heart, indifferent to the *schlachta* title, he tossed out those rat-gnawed red boots, which had always seemed to him faintly ridiculous.

He kept a copy of Emi's photo in his billfold, the original safe in his desk. His dreams were still visited by a long-lost girl who wandered the snowbound streets of a winter city somewhere in Hapsburg Europe—not the same, of course, but not altogether different from that girl leaning out her window to regale a goose.

Sometimes as in espionage films she awaited him at dusk under a streetlight on the corner—"the girl in the raincoat," as he thought of her, high-pointed French collar turned up against the wind and cold, and war and fate, no doubt, into the bargain. In some fire-bright café, sipping golden cognac from fine crystal glasses, they explored each other's eyes and hearts without a word. And awakening during the night, he would cling to her fleeting image long enough to trace its thread back down the tunnels of sweet sleep into his dream.

Where had they gone, those lovers? Out into the snow, of course, and onward into the night city; he saw them from afar in passage down snow-silenced streets to a thatched cottage. And he was welcomed into her fresh bed, where an oddly unerotic episode commenced as he awoke.

EIGHT

Next morning at the Christian service, upset because she has forgotten to bring the small crucifix for the token altar, Sister Ann-Marie grabs up a charred scrap of plywood from the railbed and gouges a crude cross into the platform gravel, then slings her tool aside in a rough gesture that seems disrespectful not only of the Cross but of this small shivering congregation and perhaps even the martyrs they are here to honor. Her gouged symbol desecrates the last steps of those prisoners who were herded up this platform toward the Golgotha of those waiting woods—or so, Olin suspects, Sister Catherine might be thinking.

"Please take more care, Sister," Catherine reproves her in an undertone. In response, the culprit wrenches the silver crucifix from her own throat, snapping its chain, then thrusts crucifix and prayer book at the other before plunging her face into her hands and sinking to her knees with a torn sobbing.

Bending to murmur into her ear, Sister Catherine urges her to rise at once. The girl only blubbers, face twisted, inconsolable, and despite his pity, Olin finds himself repelled by the heavy moles on her pasty skin, the unpowdered acne and moustache, the red eyes puffy with self-pity.

The lot of very plain young women has always struck him as monstrously unjust. What spark missing from the eyes, the smile, what scent or fleshly chemistry, could make such a fatal difference in two faces whose cast of feature, to a blind man's touch, might be identical? The two might share similar natures, biologies, desires, capabilities, the same urgent drive to be passionately wanted and to love and procreate. Yet one will be set aside by a mere gene, some minute strand of protoplasm undetectable by the known senses, that condemns her to an unfulfilled existence—unless, that is, she should happen to be spared by an unusual intelligence or wit or lively manner of the sort so lacking in poor Ann-Marie.

Like most men, he has carelessly assumed that such misfortune is what impels a young woman to commit heart and mind and yearning body to the nun's barren calling, with only the love of poor emaciated Christ to see her through. He pities this girl truly. Yet at this moment, even so, he is annoyed that this creature has embarrassed Sister Catherine. When Ann-Marie can't be coaxed onto her feet, he steps behind her, reaches down and locates her soft armpits and with a great surge of distaste heaves the dead weight of her up off the gravel.

Taken aback by Olin's intervention, Sister Catherine waves away another man who has stepped forward to help; she does this so brusquely that the man raises his eyebrows, then permits himself a sort of smile when a moment later, as she attempts to assist Olin from the other side, the two bump foreheads in the act of lifting.

"I've never bumped heads with a nun before," Olin whispers. He laughs quietly and she bites her lip, then gives in to a bright peal of girlish mirth that charms him—that in fact delights him, though he senses how close her laughter comes to the frantic laughter of an overtired child up past its bedtime that may shatter in wails from one moment to the next: for whatever reason, this young Catherine is in despair. Observing them, Ann-Marie decides she is being mocked—*"Oh!"*—and is instantly up there on the Cross with Jesus; twisting free, she rushes off the ramp and on across the snowy tracks, bound for the fence and the nearest gate that might lead to a place of refuge in the women's compound.

Sister Catherine does not call after her. She considers the misshapen cross—"the *wound*," she murmurs in a small queer voice—then distances herself from it a little before leading a bare service with no altar.

Just as well Priest Mikal is absent, Olin supposes, exchanging a wry look with the man who tried to help. He had not recognized the ex-monk Stefan, whose fur hat conceals the monk's tonsure encircling his scalp like a fallen halo.

Sister Catherine whispers to her group that under ordinary circumstances, Sister Ann-Marie would never permit herself to behave in such a manner. As an unsophisticated peasant girl taught by country priests, she is naturally upset by the shock of her first exposure to a death camp and also certain anti-papist rants which have made a painful situation that much worse. She does not have to say that for a devout novice, the discovery that failed Catholics were prominent among those responsible for Auschwitz-Birkenau has been excruciating.

Catherine herself looks harried, as if at any moment she might sink into a heap as the other girl had done, simply unravel. "Yet you have borne it," he reminds her.

"Yes," she says, looking around to see if the missing sister might have reappeared. "These days we must persevere, try to see clearly. There are decisions."

What sort of decisions? For Sister Catherine? For the Church? Surely something more urgent than Earwig's abuse is badly troubling her. Even if she won't confide in him, he wants to engage her in some way, tease her a little, to lighten the atmosphere between them. *Stop inspecting her! Where are your manners?* But really, how *alive* she looks in her distress, almost pretty in her way, even in heavy black habit. He checks an absurd impulse to reach out and lightly touch her cheek. *Want to bless her or something? You're ridiculous!*

Olin says, "I was just wondering why Priest Mikal doesn't attend your services." "He is not our priest," she says too sharply, "and anyway, he can't be everywhere: no doubt he has duties to attend to at the church."

"I'll just go have a look for Ann-Marie," he tells her. "*Sister* Ann-Marie," she says, plainly regretting the entire unsuitable exchange.

When Sister Catherine and the others return to the circle, Olin stays behind to kick at the mutilated cross with his boot toe, trying to smooth it. Stefan has lingered, too, apparently entertained by his frustration, but Olin soon quits, in a hurry to catch up, nodding to Stefan curtly as he passes. When he glances back a minute later, the man has already set off in the opposite direction, toward the tunnel.

OLIN LEAVES THE CIRCLE after the first meditation period and makes his way across the tracks and through the fence into the women's compound. (By what warped code were the sexes kept strictly separate while awaiting death?) In one of these preserved barracks lived Tadeusz Borowski's beloved fiancée Maria, arrested with him. In another, Dr. Mengele performed his hideous experiments on twin children. And somewhere here—this haunts him—a wistful child scrawled on the wall: "No butterflies live here." This river lowland must have breathed mosquito clouds in warmer weather when every last butterfly, beetle, worm, and spider was devoured on sight by the famished prisoners, and the root of the poorest weed. Once the grass was gone and the river rose in rain and flood, mud oozed over these floors; in the dry summer, the prisoners choked on the hot dust, hallucinating in the dream of water.

Each barrack held seven hundred women and a few children in the animal reek of small tight rooms. He locates the fading crayon drawings depicting a schoolhouse and some happy kids pulling a hobbyhorse and a toy dog—the famous "children's paintings," so poignant in their effort to be cheerful, whose height above the floor suggests that they were actually the work of mothers desperate to help starving children through those endless hours.

Alone in the last of the bare rooms, he calls out to the missing Ann-Marie. Nobody answers. Fearing the scrape and whisper of thin shoes, he retreats outside to find his breath.

⁂

THAT AFTERNOON, Olin walks into the town, armed only with a surname and his precious snapshot of that dark-haired girl leaning out of her thatched window. The melancholy nature of his quest and its high likelihood of failure—are these the real reasons he has put this off? Nobody is left at home who might hold him to account; they hadn't wanted him to come here in the first place. Yet he feels a peculiar obligation to the girl in the photo, and perhaps a vague responsibility to his late father as well. And he also needs the knowledge that he tried.

With no realistic ambition, then, beyond putting a duty behind him, he locates the town hall–courthouse on the square. Here nobody, it seems, much wants to help a nosy foreigner hunting through old records, a stranger speaking archaic Polish and quite possibly intent on bringing more notoriety to their town. Next he walks the streets on the lookout for some older citizen who might point him toward a neighborhood where another elder might recall that name or recognize the window of the old thatched house in his photo or even, impossibly, the girl herself. *Could that be our young schoolteacher? The old doctor's daughter?* But knowing the unlikelihood of any such encounter, he only feels more aimless and depressed.

The few pedestrians in the shabby streets look poisoned by a stranger's cordial smile and deaf to his greetings. Windows appear tight shut all over town. But rumors must have flown before him, for on the next corner four men stop to stare in a hard knot of closed faces. After a consultation, they turn toward him, forming a loose line that does not quite bar his way.

His greeting is met with suspicion and his queries mocked doltishly, with feigned incomprehension. The guy in front, a bareheaded man in a red scarf, hands jammed into torn pockets of his scruffy jacket, pretends that the stranger's accent is outlandish, unfathomable; another masticates the name he seeks, turning it over and over on his tongue as one might test a suspect mushroom. Finally, with a small stiff bow, Olin turns his back on their hard raillery, retreats the way he came. Wandering around town this way is useless. His mind assures him he has done his duty, so why won't his heart tell him he has done his best?

On his return, Olin is startled to be hailed cheerily by a girl's voice: he turns to see Mirek's pretty Wanda in an upstairs window. "Baron Olinski!"—can that be what she said? Before he can respond, she is summoned rudely by a voice somewhere within; a quick wave, then the smile is gone and does not reappear.

GLAD TO BE FINISHED with Oswiecim, he is curious to see what might have become of that part of the estate indicated on his old family map of Brzezinka village and environs which he'd compared with the chart in the museum; it appears to be located beyond the farther crematoria, in an outlying area of the vast camp.

Georgie Earwig, suffering sore knees, readily abandons meditation and uninvited tags along when Olin follows the path through the low wood that separates Crematoriums #3 and #4 from the fallow winter fields outside the fences.

Beyond the wood, a storm-split tree stands by itself in a long meadow of thick high grasses that according to his map might have belonged to the estate. On the camp chart, this meadow seems to be the site of a mass grave used when the overloaded ovens fell behind schedule: is it only his imagination that under these heavy grasses glazed with ice the ground is soft, unstable, that it quakes in a sickening way beneath his boots like a great grassy jelly? His companion steps gingerly as if he, too, had noticed that in this place the very ground is rotten.

They do not speak of it, nor even mutter, until well clear of that meadow. But the unspeakable experience weakens their defenses, and Olin risks a rude retort by asking where the other man was born. He means, *Who the hell are you, anyway? Why are you here?* Earwig only shakes him off. He growls but does not answer.

⁂

AFTER THE WAR, the escaped prisoner Stanislav K., or "K" as he is known, self-identified as the only fugitive from Auschwitz-Birkenau never recaptured, became a folksinger of medieval ballads in Warsaw. In a strange "homesick-ness" mysterious even to himself, K keeps returning in old age; he camps in an unheated room in Auschwitz I, even sets out winter seed for little birds.

Olin's Polish friends, who knew K in his Warsaw days, have invited him to come this evening to tell his story.

Like the artist Malan and other brave boys and young men, K fled the Nazi invasion in the fall of 1939 and headed for France to join what was left of the Polish army. Arrested with four comrades as they crossed Slovakia, he'd been turned over to the Gestapo and trucked to Auschwitz, where even in those early days, K says, the smallest misstep or neglect of a detail was a matter of life or death. "It was mad and it was terrible," he sighs, a bit theatrically, "and human beings designed it."

Here in Auschwitz I, in those first years, the bodies of Polish prisoners could be retrieved for burial by their families. K recalls a young SS guard at the main gate, smiling and whistling as he checked the coffins, slipping an ice pick from his boot and pushing it casually through the heart of each cadaver to make sure no prisoner escaped by playing dead, then returning to his booth, still whistling, still smiling. "'Lili Marlene,'" K says. "Always 'Lili Marlene,' over and over and over."

In those early days, it was permitted to write letters home, although the SS destroyed them. K still seems astonished that the Jewish prisoners, unlike the Poles, made no effort to send Christmas greetings to their families. "Jews don't celebrate Christmas, for Christ's sake," a harsh voice informs him. "And anyway, they had no family to send greetings to because any family still alive was in here with them."

In the late spring of 1942, when K's work party ran off through the woods behind the crematoria, most were killed quickly or recaptured and hanged before the assembled prisoners. K survived by running all night through the forest and lying down at dawn in a deep furrow in a field of new green grain. Covering himself with soil, he lay in that furrow like a dead man for two nights, three days—"right out in the open, where nobody thought to look," grins this old man, still boyishly delighted—before he was discovered by a farm girl. The girl crept back after dark and led him home, and because her brother had been murdered by the Gestapo, her mother vowed to save this young man instead.

One hundred fellow prisoners were hanged as a consequence of K's escape, Zygmunt the sculptor whispers to Olin, looking cross when Olin refers to the moral burden this old man must carry. K himself shows no sign of any burden, nor does he mention the executed prisoners. Instead he observes that he survived only because he was a hardy Pole blessed by his Christian faith: no Jew tried to escape this place, he informs his mostly Jewish audience, because "as everyone knows," Jews are not fighters like the Poles but a weaker and more passive race, bending their necks to their fate.

Gratuitous insult, incorrigible Polish prejudice! A young rabbi jumps up with righteous commotion and storms out. The speaker has ignored the fact, calls an angry voice, that the odds were somewhat better for escaping Poles than for fugitive Jews crossing hostile landscapes in zebra-striped tunics without food or water, knowledge of the language, or sane destination. And how about that famous rebellion at Treblinka? And the Warsaw uprising in which Jews of the Polish underground were leaders—?

Trying to ease matters, Ben Lama reminds K's audience that theirs will be the last generation that can truly say, We have heard the firsthand witness of survivors—witness all the more important, he adds, at a time when neo-Nazis and malignant others are yelping more stridently than ever that "the so-called Holocaust" has been greatly exaggerated if indeed it had ever occurred. Once the last of these firsthand witnesses are gone, this villainous lie will only spread.

Unmollified, many Jews complain next day that none of the retreat leaders rose to protest K's offensive remarks except that one young rabbi who marched out. K's friends concede that the brave old man might have been untactful about what is, after all, a well-known behavioral distinction; from their point of view, a national hero has been repaid with ingratitude for coming to contribute his hard experience to their clearly very limited understanding.

NINE

At her request, Olin shows Catherine the proofs of his new anthology of verse by Herbert and Milosz and Szymborska and other great modern writers of her country: as a group, he says, only the Polish poets rival the modern Americans as the finest in the world today.

In their discussion of the poems, Catherine mentions that her namesake, St. Catherine of Siena, that gentle Dominican of the fourteenth century, had been a poet.

"'All the way to Heaven is Heaven,'" Olin smiles, and she raises her brows in pleased surprise, gratified that a nonbeliever can quote St. Catherine's sublime teaching. And though he fears he may be making a mistake, he can't help mentioning an apocryphal parable that seems to express St. Catherine's teaching in a darker way.

Christ crucified is importuned by a penitent thief, in
agony on his own cross on that barren hillside. "I beseech
you, Jesus, take me with you this day to Paradise!" In traditional gospels, Jesus responds, "Thou shalt be with me this
day in Paradise," but in older texts—Eastern Orthodox or
the Apocrypha, perhaps?—Christ shakes his head in pity,
saying, "No, friend, we are in Paradise right now."

She stares at him.

"No hope of Heaven," he says gently. "No Trinity, no
Resurrection. All Creation right here now."

"That is not our idea of things," she says evenly, retreating among his pages. And when he asks if while she reads
he might glance over her notes from yesterday's meditation,
she passes him her diary without looking at him.

> . . . *the prisoners are hurrying in fear of death, yet I*
> *hear faint voices. They are singing . . .*

Oh Lord, those wandering souls again, with their infer-
nal singing! Her stuff is strong but it is also sentimental, a
bit "poetical," he thinks. As metaphor, her voices from on
high might have some merit if so many of their companions
weren't also tuning into them in their platform meditations.
Some even report a tinkling of little bells in the winter
sky—the music of the spheres, perhaps? Some weird acous-
tical contagion?

To spare them both the strain of a forced compliment,

he returns her diary with a wordless bow that he trusts might convey the sincere respect of one poet for another, but feels duplicitous when it seems to work. In that sudden smile of hers is a gleam of fresh white teeth and breathless innocence. *My God, man, what's got into you? You'd like to kiss her, right? You're a damned fool, Olin. Truly.*

TEN

The skeletal caretaker staff at Auschwitz I stays mostly out of sight; Auschwitz II at Birkenau shows no sign of life whatever. The long two-story building flanking the Gate stands gaunt and empty. At Auschwitz-Birkenau there is no conceivable Borowski research to be done nor any real reason to remain. So when Ben Lama inquires amiably how his work is progressing, he can only say that something feels unfinished.

This evening that big woman "from the other side" appears again, and this time Olin stands nearby and translates her rude dialect into English. This woman does not associate with Olin's coven of educated Poles (nor, he feels sure, would she be welcome) and takes no part in the mess hall conversations, bringing her own rough food in a sack and devouring it without interest on a concrete bench out in the courtyard. A local peasant, Rebecca's friend Nadia decides, nodding her head with a tolerant smile and a cold eye of unabashed intolerance.

Granite-faced, eyes aimed straight at the wall behind their heads, the woman forces out her words between hard pauses. "I think . . . I am a natural oppressor. I *know* I am. I would be good at it." Braving the shocked silence, she states this flatly without trying to excuse it, yet spits up years of bitterness about the beatings and sexual abuse endured in childhood at the hands of a drunkard father, then the batterings and rape by a drunkard husband; sarcastic, she asks "you educated people" if there might be some connection. She declares she has no sympathy for the people killed here except for those few who fought back.

One night, in a dream that recurred often, she found herself among naked wailing women being pushed and packed "like sausage meat" into the gas chamber. Though she fought like an animal—"I bit them," she says—she could not keep her footing in the tide of bodies and went under.

"That's when I woke up. I was very surprised to be alive." With a ragged cough, she points in the direction of the town. "I live all my life in my dark hole over there. As a little kid, I saw the black smoke rising. I have come here many times and I feel nothing, nothing. I feel nothing to-night. But here I am again, okay? So *why?*" She glares around the room. "Can you tell me why I must come back, and back again?" Like K and Malan, Olin reflects. Is this the same weird longing?

Despite her torment, she is too honest to pretend she is troubled by late-life compassion for the victims, nor does she feel the least sympathy with their mission, and because she refuses to give ground, even those who recoil from her are stirred. In consequence, in a spontaneous response that no one can quite fathom, her listeners seek to comfort her as she flees the hall. Olin's temples prickle strangely when women reach out to touch her as she blunders toward the exit, plainly mortified by her own tears and fighting to re-press the jagged grin that cracks her raw red face.

OUTSIDE THE AUDITORIUM, "Big Erna," as Anders calls her, waylays Olin. She has learned from neighbors that a Polish-speaking foreigner has been snooping around town inquiring about some long-forgotten family. "You?" She points a bony finger at his eyes. (Is that the harsh odor of her hairy armpits or just old boiled cabbage?) In what he takes to be clumsy appreciation of her warm reception a few minutes earlier, she declares her intent to assist him in his search, which he then confesses he has already abandoned; after so many years, he says, any such quest seems hopeless.

That he may have seized on an excuse to give up out of some fear of succeeding occurs to him in the same moment it occurs to her. Big Erna is openly suspicious. Absolutely some elder can be found who will recall the family. In those days, Oswiecim was a small market town "where everyone was neighbors" and the name of an established doctor would be common knowledge. "We search," she grumbles. Shown the photo, she becomes excited: there might be just such a thatched house in the older neighborhoods behind the square: after all, there are not so many left. Nostrils twitching, she is already on the hunt.

Next morning he is marched by Erna past the Hotel Glob and on across the small central square of low dull buildings and scrawny Cold War shop fronts and that faded yellow courthouse on the corner. In a side street leading downhill toward the river—and she points—stands her Roman church; over there somewhere—that backhand wave of upswept fingers seems dismissive—is the last of the five synagogues that once served the old Jewish community. "What? Five, yes, why not? This was a Jew town: maybe two out of three Jewish." She whinnies in triumph when he looks astonished. "Many cemeteries," she adds as they turn the corner. "Polish, German, Russian—many dead here. Old Jew cemetery, too, but nobody takes care of it."

"Maybe nobody left to tend it."

"Yes, maybe nobody," she agrees. "Only the weeds." Even those few who returned after the war were expelled in 1968. "This time Communists," she adds as if to say, *Who knows who will come hunting those Jews next?* "And our priests cooperated with the secret police, same way they did with the Gestapo." She shrugs, indifferent. "Rumors, rumors. But that's what people say."

Standing before an old unpainted house, they compare it to what may be seen of the thatched dwelling in the photo and agree that it may be the same. Flushed from his cottage next door by Big Erna, who spotted him skulking behind curtains, an aged neighbor confirms that this decrepit place was once the fine home of the doctor. "That is correct. Allgeier was his name." The old man's wife has crept outside behind him, already complaining that her husband like the rest of those young boys was always sniffing after the Allgeier daughter, the pretty schoolteacher. Shown the photo, she cries, "Oh Lord, that's her! She went away!"

The old man nods. After the Allgeiers disappeared, he says, the Olinskis' lawyer moved right in. "Informer, they say. Collaborator. Never moved out till they carried him out. Started to stink, I guess."

"Those people never came back," his woman sighs, uneasy. These old people, exchanging glances, seem to know something about Erna that they don't much like. Erna ignores this. Her nudge is heavy: *Ask!*

But having noticed Erna's nudge, the old people grow

wary and retreat indoors. "Never came back? Why?" Olin calls after them, already knowing, hoping they won't answer.

⁂

HE IS SILENT on the walk back to the square. She feeds his dread. "Funny thing, we never see those old red wooden boxcars anymore." He snaps at her too quickly, "That's just talk. Who really knows what happened to her?" And the woman's sneer says, *Suit yourself.*

He is embarrassed that their search proved to be so simple and relieved when his guide quits him at the corner where, just down the street, her dark red church thrusts up from its grove of small black winter trees. "Satisfied, Baron?" she inquires.

Baron? Hadn't Wanda said that, too? He had talked too much, arriving in Oswiecim. Then, this morning, he had mentioned to this Erna woman that the "estate agent" referred to by those old people had been an unprincipled lawyer for his family. A grunt was her one comment. She already knew.

In no need of thanks, Erna is off to help welcome the new priest transferred here by his bishop from a parish north of Warsaw near Treblinka. "Let's hope he's not one of *those*!" she calls over her shoulder. "One of which?" he calls back, disingenuous. She emits a loud bark devoid of mirth.

Miss Emmeline Allgeier, schoolteacher. Throughout his youth, that name was scarcely mentioned. Eventually, his father married, then the old Baron died. On his last visit to his grandmother, he found her semi-comatose, disputing someone in her head. Was there anything he could bring her? Slowly opening her loose old eyes, sardonic to the last, she croaked thickly, "Bring me death," then closed her eyes and seemingly withdrew into her coma. He had risen, on the point of leaving, when her voice said briskly, "I suppose the mother might have had some Jew in her. Hard to tell about those people."

He sat down again, in silence. "You should have told me, Grandmother," he said finally. Her eyes opened so quickly he had to believe the old cobra had known from the start that he was right there by the bed. Invigorated now, she actually sat up a little.

"Now why on earth would we burden you with such a story, David, even if we thought it might be true? Why on earth would you ever wish to know?"

"Grandmother? What are you saying here—?" He took a deep breath. "Is she dead or isn't she?"

"Dead?"

Never before had he dared speak to her in such a tone. The old woman shrank back as if whipped across the face.

Not that she retreated, far less tried to reassure him. What she said was, "Don't be silly, David. How would I know?" *What possible difference can it make to me when I'm as good as dead myself?* "No, no, it's that other matter I'd worry about if I were you, boy. The Jewess. But of course," she continued, "that's long forgotten, David, no one need ever know. I mean, you *look* all right, tall and fair and almost as handsome as your father in your way. No one would suspect a thing. So you needn't mope or go snooping about, pestering people. You don't have to be 'David,' that's all I'm saying."

You look all right. You don't have to be David—he never forgot a word. Nor could he ever quite forgive that death-bed vengeance wreaked on him for bringing suspect blood into the family. *So you needn't go snooping about in Poland,* that was there, too. That had always been there, like her unfailing use of "David" in association with any mention of his mother. How naive he'd been, that awful moping little David! But afterward he could not be sure what she was really saying. Was it just possible that Emi Allgeier was still alive?

In the end, he felt deeply frustrated and bitter but also very sad about the absence in his boyhood of all boyhood's robust aspects and events—the *fun* of all that running and shouting out in the wild joy of bursting forth, the rushing to welcome every moment of his life, the games and excursions, the presents and those birthday parties celebrated by other children ("Birthday party? But we don't *know* your birth date, dear, you see?"), the solace of warm loving hugs, safe sanctuary: even apes had that much, Anders said. What had always been missing was a true bond with others, women especially, and perhaps also with himself. Apart from a few unremarkable poems and some modest distinction as a scholar, who in hell was he?

⁂

HE NEEDS TO SORT OUT crumpled feelings before joining the others at Birkenau; perhaps he'll feel better if he pays his respects at what may have been the final station of his mother's cross. The last prisoners in the Cracow ghetto, he has read, were transported to Auschwitz-Birkenau in August 1942, so Emmeline Allgeier and her mother and young sister (known as "Peek," according to his father) would have arrived before the railway was extended through the tunnel into the camp and the platforms built to accommodate the horde of Jewish prisoners from Greece and Hungary. Before that, they would have been off-loaded at the original terminal, the so-called *Judenrampe*, which must still be out there in the buffer zone between the *Lager* and the town. Somewhere a spur must branch off from the main line; the junction can't be very far from where this farm road crosses the tracks.

Just beyond that point, he follows a broken disused road that roughly parallels the tracks; it passes north along a wall of thorn and bramble, emerging eventually in an abandoned railway yard of frost-split broken concrete paving and wind-banged rusty sheds. Here, sure enough, a spur splits off from the main line in the direction of the *Lager*. In the fork, still monitoring the junction, stands what looks like a defunct whistle-stop, a nondescript blockhouse of dirty industrial concrete with one cobwebbed broken window.

Across the yard where the spur disappears into the over-growth, he enters a narrow lane between walls of thicket. Glimpsed through the branch tops, a slow freight rumbles past on the main line. Farther on, around a wooded bend, the lane skirts a cluster of knocked-down dwellings over-whelmed by weed trees, saplings, hawthorne—presumably one of the condemned rural communities in the no-man's-land surrounding the new camp, torn down and scavenged by those famished prisoners for its wood and bricks. Not far beyond, the spur reappears on open ground—the origi-nal terminus, the *Judenrampe*. On the tracks, still coupled, stand two short-bodied red cattle cars, darkened by weather.

The wooden cars sit oddly high above the platform (the children, he thinks, and the elderly and the disabled must have landed hard) and the bolted doors evoke at once the doors in the SS photographs of the disgorged cargos, the confused figures amidst piles of old suitcases and bundles and the knapsacked children whose yellow stars, deathly white in those old prints, loom so large on the dark suits of those little boys wearing neckties and knickers, the better to make a favorable impression at their destination.

☼

Not a stone's throw from the cattle cars, a sulphur-yellow cottage with orange-red tile roof squats on bare clay. On its farther side, a brick patio still under construction has a matchless prospect of Birkenau's main tower, a mile away across low swampy ground crisscrossed by crows. The entrance, like a huge black grotto at this distance, looks more than ever like a cave. In the early days, in every weather, the doomed were driven all that way across that mile on foot, ragged lines of reeling figures dragging those last precious belongings they'd been ordered to bring with them. On some unknown date, perhaps not long after his own safe arrival in North America, Emi Allgeier and her mother and her little sister Peek must have walked that road.

A young man clutching a blueprint appears around the corner of the house, and seeing Olin, grins. But Olin turns on him, exclaiming, "My God, man, why in hell would you wish to live in such a place?" He is pointing at the Cave, the tower, the red wall.

The young man stares at this intruder who dares berate

him in archaic Polish. His face closes. Stolid, he considers the death camp tower and the gate.

"Mirek? Oh hell. Listen, I'm sorry."

"Because it's cheap," says Mirek. He points at a second cottage under construction in the trees beyond. "Good mortgages out here, too." He rolls up his blueprint, heads for the other house, not looking anymore at the guest of Poland.

⁂

FROM THE *JUDENRAMPE,* the rails disappear into thorn thicket. Finding no path, he walks an earthen dike across the meadow to the new paved road from Oswiecim that comes to the *Lager* by way of a high bridge over the tracks farther down the line. This dike crossing the low ground must be the path taken by his mother and her terrified family, and this *knowing* undoes him, striking down the last of his dispassion.

Emerged from the tunnel, he hurries down the endless platform, gaining on the stragglers as they draw near the memorial terrace between crematoria. From a distance, seen through the gauze of a light snowfall, those dark amorphous figures trudging in that same direction might be the prisoners of long ago, herded toward the wood.

LEADING THEM THROUGH the broken gate of #2's steel fence, the beatific cantor Rabbi Dan is singing in sweet tenor a hymn adapted from the Psalms, *"Pitkhu li shaarei tzedek; avo bam, odeh Yah . . ."* Whispering, Adina translates for Olin's benefit ("Open for me the Gates of Righteousness, I will enter through and praise the Lord") as they make their way around the ruin to join a service on the farther side. Invoking the Prayer for the Dead, the congregants surround a rain-filled pit which after fifty years of weather is a greasy pool heavily matted with green-yellow duckweed. Into this pit in the early days, so he has read, the ash produced daily in this single building from an estimated fourteen thousand corpses was dumped before a market for commercial fertilizer could be developed. ("A criminal waste," hisses Earwig, tossing a scrap of brick into the pond. But he has sense enough today to mutter his ironies under his breath.)

Apparently Father Mikal has forsaken his welcome in Oswiecim to attend this ceremony. On behalf of a Jewish-Christian reconciliation society in Warsaw, he steps forward to express stiff formal hope that their ecumenical retreat in this "Golgotha," as His Holiness called it on the great occasion of his visit, will help to heal any last schisms between faiths in "our new Poland." He spreads his arms wide in blessing as the congregation murmurs in approval, and appears discomfited when Sister Catherine steps forward unbidden as soon as he steps back. Olin and Adina exchange a worried glance: the novice's intense expression signals her opinion that the priest's pro forma speech at the ash pit of Birkenau's main crematorium had been inadequate.

The novice sinks onto her knees in the wet snow. In a taut voice, hands lifted in prayer, she begs the Lord's mercy for those Christian Poles who abetted the oppressors in their hideous cruelties to the Jewish people and the sinful indifference of those high prelates of the Church who knew the truth, yet out of prejudice and cowardice and—worst of all—indifference, failed to protest or attempt to intervene.

Here Sister Ann-Marie forsakes her with a chirrup of dismay, roiling the congregation in the commotion of her flight, but Georgie Earwig, a rare grin lighting his face, is raising clasped hands above his head, and even austere Adina Schreier smiles approval as Catherine, glancing just once at the priest, concludes in a resolute pure voice, "In coming here, may we humbly offer our great sorrow that this dreadful thing was done by Christians in a Christian country."

The priest glides forward to hover like an avenging angel at a point just off her shoulder; he bends low to speak into her ear. But surely he must know from her demeanor, Olin thinks, that not even a papal edict would suffice to still that voice.

In the silence, Olin lifts his hands, thinking to defend her with applause, but her eyes have found him and her bleak gaze stays him. *I am destroyed*, it says. For a near minute, head sinking to her breast, she remains kneeling in the snow. At the very least, she has gone too far and has frightened herself badly.

A year ago, according to Adina (who has picked the simple brain of Ann-Marie), Catherine was suspended from her teaching ministry and her novitiate for questioning the papal ban against the ordination of women priests. Under the terms of her provisional reinstatement, this public criticism of the priest entrusted with her spiritual guidance makes her vulnerable to another bad report. And this from a man, Olin has noticed, who during his own prayer never touched knee to the muddy ground and is now retreating into the congregation as if to separate himself from a heretic's ravings.

Rising at last, Sister Catherine is approached by Moishe T., the lone *Ostjude* survivor. Tottering forward, the lachrymose old man takes her hands and peers into her eyes for second after second before turning to the gathering without releasing her. In a thin, scratched voice, he testifies that what he has just heard is the first heartfelt repentance from a Roman Catholic he has experienced in all the years since his own deliverance from hell fifty years before.

When finally old Moishe lets go and moves away, Catherine stands motionless, pale and trembling in the cold, as if a wand must be waved or an ogre slain to break the spell and set her free. Olin longs to go forward and hug her. *Hey, great idea, boy! Go make things worse for her, why don't you?*

Now Priest Mikal is there again. Ignoring the novice, he raises his palms high to command attention, then asks permission to correct a certain inference made here today, that most Catholics in Poland collaborated in the Nazi evil. On the contrary, he says, drawing a paper from his pocket, many would have agreed with the spirit of this leaflet circulated in Warsaw in September 1942, when the stain of a huge genocide was already spreading through the West. That he quotes it from memory suggests to Olin that he has resorted to it often.

The world observes this crime more terrible than any seen by history—and it is silent. The massacre of millions of defenseless people is taking place amid a universal, ominous silence. He who does not condemn condones! We do not have the means to act against the German murderers, we can save no one, but we protest! This protest is demanded of us by God.

The brave young Catholic who risked her life was imprisoned here in late 1943 but was freed by Russian soldiers a year later: her miraculous survival should be understood

by persons of true faith, adds Priest Mikal, as a manifestation of the Lord's great mercy.

ALREADY SHAKEN by his morning in Oswiecim, then the
Judenrampe, Olin finds himself painfully distracted by a
cold draught from the direction of the fallen wing of the
crematorium, some forty yards off to his left; it pierces his
clothing on that side, chilling his skin under the armpit as
if his parka had been slit by a knife of ice.

Uneasy, he remains behind as Rabbi Dan concludes the
service at the ash pit and the others drift away. Then he
turns—he *feels turned*, rather—toward that concrete tum-
ble he has shunned instinctively since his arrival. He can
neither withdraw that blade of ice nor set the pain aside as
morbid or absurd: if anything, it has intensified, like the
hard bite of winter in his frozen boots.

Unsteady, he draws near the ruin. In some cranny of his
brain, he thinks, this place has awaited him all his life, ever
since those nightmares of his boyhood.

Only the far end of the cellar chamber lies exposed. The
rest is filled by huge tilted slabs pierced by rusted rods
hard-twisted in the explosion by the falling mass of concrete. Behind the crematorium, over there in that thin
wood, poor naked Emi, dragged at by her howled-out little

sister, must have stumbled forward on numb lacerated feet at the shouted order, arms crossed over her breasts, hunched down so that her elbows might shield the dark patch of her pubis from the greedy cameras.

He retreats into his parka hood and pulls its throat cord tight against the cold, against the phantasms and spirits—the "wandering souls" of Sister Catherine, the hungry ghosts (Ben Lama and his Buddhists), the horde of the lost inhabiting the emptiness of this flat river plain in Poland. But inevitably he succumbs to the terrifying vision of that young woman seeking to hush her gnashing mother, shriek her love to the child clasped to her thigh as naked as a frog in the press of cold-fleshed bodies as more and more are packed in with them, giving off queer heat; gone wild, she fights to save her dear ones from being drawn under in the crush and suffocation.

The iron door, slamming, smashes feet and clawing fingers. A crack of light as, jammed by arms, the door reopens for a moment, is slammed again and bolted—that *clang* perhaps the signal to executioners overhead peeping filthily as demons as they seed the pandemonium below with white cyanide pellets dumped from black-and-orange canisters—this, perhaps, in those very moments when her baby was being dandled in the New World. He can't get past this nor can he escape the screams and coughs of violent gagging, the raw stench as fluids spatter, the bursting eyes of the mad creatures below this rim where Emi's only begotten child kneels shuddering a half century later. In the death struggle for the last exhausted air, the strongest clamber onto piles of weaker, and the young woman shrieks back at her voiceless sister as Peek is drawn beneath the human biomass that wipes her stare, the round hole of her mouth from the face of earth.

⁂

DID HE BLACK OUT? How long has he crouched here on the cellar rim, on the point of vomiting, and so close to the edge that he must reach back and grab his bootheels so as not to topple in?

Regaining his feet, he staggers to find balance. He totters past the ash pit, peering about him until finally he locates those clumped figures far off down the platform toward the Gate. Dazed, he makes his way to the meditation circle, where he is overwhelmed at once by that silence of dead centuries and a universal solitude far lonelier than any he might ever have imagined.

⁂

TOWARD DUSK, a weeping German woman leads the circle in a lullaby for the slain children. *Guten Abend, gute*

Nacht / Mit Rosen bedacht. The voices are tentative and shy at first, a low whispery singing, and some sniffle.

On the long trudge back to Auschwitz I, Olin is still slow and unsteady, and people peer at him as they pass by. Without turning, he is presently aware of Catherine overtaking, drawing near, with the chastened Sister Ann-Marie somewhere behind.

Now she walks beside him. He looks pale, she murmurs. Is he all right? "Well, I have felt better, it is true." Still entangled in that ruin, his thought is jumbled and his voice hollow, faraway. In truth, he has no very clear idea how he is feeling—he feels quite literally *beside* himself, and has to concentrate to compose his face into some semblance of alert human expression.

To keep her close, he asks her to translate the last lines of that German lullaby sung on the platform. "Goodness," she murmurs, "that sweet lullaby in such a place." In this region of Hapsburg-Austrian culture, she reminds him, most of the educated Jews moaned their last prayers in the language of their executioners: even those who had no German surely knew this verse and sang it to the frightened children: *Early in the morning, God willing, you shall awaken; early in the morning, God willing, you shall awaken.*

Trying to cheer them both, he teases her. "I suppose those voices singing in the snowfall remind you of those singing spirits you've been hearing." And this time, she smiles back. "No," she says, "mine only sing to me in Polish." However,

her smile is distracted. Across that clear face that yesterday hid nothing, dark emotions pass like shadows of bird
flight on a wall. "I am sad today," she tells him. "I think all
feel this sadness. The heaviness in this dead air—" And
she only shakes her head when he compliments her on
her speech at the ash pond. Will there be consequences? Of
course. Her words will inevitably be seen as disrespect for an
ordained priest.

Why are you still smiling in this inane way? He adjusts
his grin.

She is wary of his facetiousness: the eyes searching his
own entreat him to finish with his fooling, make his point.
"It is all very amusing, is it not?" she says, entirely unamused. Abruptly she breaks off their new rapport, such
as it is. "Please pay no attention, Dr. Olin," she instructs
him. "It is only talk." And he nods, puzzled. *What* is only
talk? She seems more open to him—is this because he looks
so needy?—but she cuts him off at once when he tries to
learn her given name and something of her past. At his
suggestion that in theory, at least, it might be nice not to
lose touch, to meet again one day after they leave here, she
squints at him as if unable to fathom why any honorable
person might want such a thing. *"Nice?"* she says. "What is
this 'nice'?" It is forbidden in her strict order, she says, to
use one's secular name or to reveal one's present whereabouts in Poland.

Before supper, still stunned by that vision at the crematorium, he must retreat outside and breathe cold air to calm himself. He needs to *be* with someone, confess something, spit out all this *feeling*. But what, precisely, is he feeling? He needs to be comforted without letting this be seen, without in fact confiding anything to anybody.

DANCING AT

AUSCHWITZ

ELEVEN

This evening the mess hall is strangely quiet. People seek corners where they won't have to talk. He touches the photograph in his shirt pocket which he won't be parted from yet cannot bear to look at; his fingertips keep drifting over to make sure that Emi is still there, still joyous in her window. When Becca plumps herself down and asks if something is the matter, he denies it. "Really, Clements? You feel fine?" She shrugs in disbelief, indicating the others. "Well, if so, you're the only one who does. This place has finished us."

Becca asks about his inquiries in Oswiecim. Too tired to dissemble, he pulls his photograph from his shirt pocket. "My mother," he says in a numb tone.

"So *pretty!*" Becca turns to appraise his face, revisits the photo. "Looks sort of Jewish, don't you think?" Returning the photo, she holds his eye. Is she teasing? Or just guessing, based on something Erna told her? He tries not to look startled, tries to smile. Shrewd Becca sorts through his expressions, sees that his eyes aren't smiling. "So," she says softly, conspiratorial. "Our dear Baron Olinski." He groans, closing his eyes to convey impatience, weariness, and also to spare himself the stress of another lie.

Mischievous Becca keeps glancing at him knowingly to make him nervous, even claims she sees a slight resemblance between the girl in his photo and "that nun you hang around." There is probing in her teasing and a note of disapproval, and his reaction is defensive. "Come on, Becca!" That's just psychiatric shoptalk, he complains, pot-stirring nonsense.

"I thought I was only joking," she says quietly. "And by the way, for somebody who feels just fine, you look just awful."

He ducks further encounters by entering the auditorium early and slipping into an empty row near the back, and so he is startled and delighted—but somehow not surprised—to be joined at the last minute by the novices. Sister Ann-Marie blunders heavily into the seat beside him, with Sister Catherine cutting off her retreat on the far side.

THIS EVENING, nobody goes forward to the stage. After these long days in the camp, depression has descended on the witness bearers like an inversion of the coal-soot fog that hangs in the outer dark of the night prison.

The tension is pervasive in the hall, as ominous as an undying echo. Needing to blame, some glare at Earwig, slouched in his usual isolation, and others at the knot of Polish men, still mired in their attitude that none of this wretched death camp business is any of their affair. *How much longer will these Jews and Germans chew at the rotten bones of their old corpse?* They seem content to ignore public condemnation. Inevitably, Becca's exasperated voice inquires, "Why did you come, then?"

FOR WANT OF WITNESS BEARERS, Ben Lama himself goes forward. Looking exhausted, he extends his opened hands for a long moment, then lets them fall again. Before the retreatants can retire to insomnia and nightmares, he tries to dispel the murk and rancor by relating the strange parable from the Old Testament that Christians call the

Dark Night of the Soul. *And Jacob, grappling in the night with the dark angel of the Unknown, cries out, I cannot let you go until you tell me your true name!* "In this place, we are all struggling with our dark angels," Ben suggests. When the parable finds no resonance among them, he summons Rabbi Dan the cantor, he of the indomitable good cheer.

Joining Ben onstage, the cantor tells an ancient tale about a man in great sorrow who worries that he does not suffer enough. "And a rabbi comforts this man in his sorrow, saying, 'The only whole heart is the broken heart. But it must be *wholly* broken.'" Smiling enigmatically (Indigestion, Olin wonders? Too many meals of cabbage soup or goulash, hard dark sour pickles, unrelenting bread?), Rabbi Dan raises his hands palms outward and repeats in a hushed whisper, "*wholly* broken," but to judge from the perplexed faces, this teaching, like Ben's parable, is not wholly understood.

The cantor draws the evening to a close by leading the congregation in *Oseh Shalom*, which he translates as "Making Peace by Making Whole." Softly, softly, swaying as he sings, blessing all with a promiscuous sweet smile, Dan summons others from both sides, taking the hands of the two nearest, who reach out to the next. Slowly at first, the linked singers move up the aisle in a clockwise direction, "making peace by making whole" all the way to the rear and on around, returning down the other aisle.

When Olin and Catherine rise to join the circle, Ann-

Marie, between them, balks; when he reaches behind him, takes her moist hand with distaste and hauls her forth, she casts a frightened glance at Father Mikal, who stands at the back wall ("keeping an eye on things for Jesus," snipes Earwig, who does not join either).

Oddly, the participants have not stopped. They continue up across the stage and down around again as if transported. Gradually shy smiles appear, a stifled giggle. Arms start to swing, then overswing, tossed high like the arms of children holding hands in schoolyard dances.

A number of celebrants look distressed that the clergy have not joined them; rather ostentatiously, a few have quit the hall. Some people who started gladly are already abandoning the circle, offering wan smiles to suggest that they'd only made a show of participation out of ecumenical solidarity until the childish folks still dancing come to their senses and realize as they have that this whole charade, if not precisely sacrilege, is bound to offend or infuriate some faith or other; it shows disrespect at the very least for the more dignified witnesses, not to mention all those martyrs being mourned.

Sister Ann-Marie's hand is twitching in his grip like a caught animal. Then it is gone, leaving him groping in the air behind. But almost at once, his hand is retrieved by small warm fingers, not Ann-Marie (who is fleeing the circle) but Sister Catherine.

In the welling of relief he feels in the intimacy of fingers, he knows that she is present, right there with him. No need to speak, no need to think, but only to be wholly present in this moment, moment after moment.

Neither the participants nor the abstainers, it seems clear, have any idea what's happening, and Olin is baffled, too, knowing only that in this simple ceremony something extraordinary is taking place, like a transfusion of elixir. What had struck him (when it didn't stop) as a sentimental self-indulgence that ordinarily he would have fled after the first round—a death camp prance of grinning fools as in some lugubrious danse macabre of the Dark Ages, enacting mankind's insignificance in the shadow of the scythe—has metamorphosed into gentle rejoicing, transcending the atmosphere of grief and banishing lamentation from the hall.

What could there be to celebrate in such a place? Who cares? He is delighted to be caught up in it. Clasping the precious hand, he just keeps moving. He moves with it, into it, and now it is moving him as the bonds of his despair relent like weary sinew and gratitude floods his heart. He feels filled with well-being, blessed, whatever "blessed" might mean to a lifelong non-believer.

Still softly singing, the remaining dancers cling to their momentum lest they lose the lift of this unholy exaltation like night insects spent in mating orbit. Then transcendence fades and the singing dies, until all at once, hands are cast away in a rush of self-consciousness, and the dance subsides into itself like a circle left on the still surface of a pond by some large form only dimly seen as it withdraws below.

Gathering new breath, nobody speaks, not yet. Then softly the silence implodes and awe arises, a sigh of bewilderment and gratitude, as with fulfilled lovers.

Olin turns to share his wonder with the novice only to find she is no longer there; she has slipped away among the milling people. In her place frets a dull changeling, Rabbi James Glock, who looks downcast amidst the eager sorting of astonishments. He had quit the circle early but apparently too late to be spared the lash of his own moral condemnation. Glaring at the beamish cantor, he is not in the least mollified when Olin comments quietly, "That was amazing, but what was it?" Says James Glock gloomily, "We'll see."

"The Rebbe Who Danced at Auschwitz! Famed in Hebrew lore!" Ben Lama giggles as he passes by, trying to tease Glock out of his indignation. Olin laughs, too, feeling gleeful. But Glock's frown only deepens, and his groan is heartfelt and profound. He moves away, too caught up in his own strife to accept comfort.

Adina Schreier is exhilarated. She nods and smiles. Finding no words for what has happened but apprehending something all the same, they open their arms and share a brisk collegial embrace without a word.

Olin and the israeli professor are invited to attend the nightly clergy meeting. There two earnest American Zen monks rush to support Rabbi Glock in deploring
that offensive "dancing" (belatedly, since both had taken
part). Adina sharply disagrees; in the Hebrew tradition,
music and dancing may express a grief too deep to be
fathomed by mere words. *Beyond, beyond, beyond all con-
solation*, she reminds them, quoting from the Mourner's
Kaddish.

From the night compound comes the plaint of the
shofar, whose mournful note Adina interprets as "a sound
from the breath of the heart, higher than reason."

The professor is feverish with inquiry. Precisely because
it was spontaneous, unanticipated, the Dancing was entirely
in keeping with the spirit of this retreat; it was inevitable,
she feels, perhaps a kind of benediction. The whole phenomenon excites her so that she has changed her mind
about quitting the retreat and returning to Israel tomorrow
and now looks forward to renewing her meditation on the
ramp in hope of insight into what just happened.

Olin is astonished to hear such wonder in the voice of
one so learned. He, too, hungers for clarification, but of
what, precisely? The mystery has not been limited to this
evening. Out on that platform at odd moments of each day,

a presence had risen that, for want of a better term, he calls "earth apprehension" in his journal—a shifting of forces, ancient and unknown, that might have originated with the first life on the planet. Could this "dancing" be a symptom of "earth apprehension"?

Dancing at Auschwitz! A diabolical idea, insists Jim Glock, the very phrase a profaning of the martyrs. Any moment now those holy ghosts at Birkenau might come thronging down around the heads of the intruders, hissing bitter prophecies and imprecations.

Dancing at Auschwitz! One hardly dares speak it aloud, Anders slyly agrees, for fear of being incinerated in one's tracks. Since the Dancing, Olin's roommate looks half-crazed, ice-blue eyes fired by his northern lights, his aurora borealis. What portent can this be?

Precisely *what* has taken place? *Something* occurred, as all who took part are eager to attest, but to call it "the Dancing" seems self-conscious and a bit trivial at the same time. In the absence of any sensible definition, "the Dancing" is inevitably reduced to "It," and reverberations of this "It" are all around them, inside, outside, everywhere.

Clements Olin is relieved that so many others will testify to "something not known to anyone at all but wild in our breast for centuries" (a favorite line from an Akhmatova poem that when quoted to Sister Catherine had evoked a gasp of enchantment, a girlish skip and clapping of the hands.

With the advent of this something-not-known (which he scarcely dares consider lest it vanish), the metastasizing animosities among the witness bearers are dissolving, as if the Dancing were sealing their acceptance of all woebegone humankind in all its greed and cruelties as the only creature capable of evil and the only one—surely these two are connected—aware that it must die.

IF ONLY IT WERE SO SIMPLE! If only there were evil people somewhere insidiously committing evil deeds, and it were necessary only to separate them from the rest of us and destroy them. But the line dividing good and evil cuts through the heart of every human being. And who is willing to destroy a piece of his own heart?

Evil as a piece of every heart—a truism no less true, he thinks, for being disputed by the righteous. When he shows Solzhenitsyn's observation to one of the Buddhist teachers, the man dismisses it as romantic or incomplete or both. "What a blessing spiritual insight is," he sighs a bit too comfortably, "which cuts through all self-lacerating partial truths while good and evil fall away." Well, yes, one could say that. But surely that old gulag survivor wrote those words not as a man blessed with spiritual insight but as the cry of a tormented being whose insight had been hard-wrung from dire suffering. How many of these humble penitents braving the weather every day all day out on that platform have been blessed with the leisure or the means to pursue a so-called "spiritual practice"? And how long would such delicate attainments have withstood the death camp's horrors?

Yes, something has happened here, is happening, will happen. Even those sophisticated Poles, who did not dance and are rather snide about the epiphanies of those who did, seem less disgruntled and even a bit humbled. And most astonishing of all, perhaps, the guilt Olin thought certain participants might suffer in the aftermath has not emerged. Is that because this phenomenon sprang forth of its own accord? He thinks so. "It" simply *was*. And those who had been open to this "It," including a few of the Orthodox Jews who might have been expected to condemn it most severely, seem not in the least plagued by doubt but on the contrary, in this atmosphere of aimless gratitude, look sort of goofily transcendent.

"Horror penetrates our bones but at the same time there is joy," says the daughter of an SS doctor. "Who would have expected joy at Auschwitz?" Her more cautious companions rush to hush such an unthinkable idea while others nod and smile in affirmation.

Or is this "joy," as Earwig and Glock and other naysayers insist, not transcendence at all but mere wishful thinking? "Superficial, unearned, irresponsible," complains Rabbi Jim, who from the outset has been self-appointed spokesman for the indignant and uneasy. That foolish Dancing, he asserts, was no more than mass hysteria born of that residue of death and darkness in the hall. Rabbi Jim's carping is so vehement that it risks being dismissed as envy of Rabbi Dan, who in his new eminence as the Rebbe Who Danced at Auschwitz is the gracious recipient of awe and deference from every side.

What had happened was no miracle, of course; nobody dares claim any such thing. But by next morning, even so, the words "miraculous" and "mystical experience" start cropping up. Together with Ben Lama and Adina, Olin worries that the force of the event will be weakened or dispersed by facile labeling, much as a rare bird might be put to flight out of the back side of a thicket by enthusiasts out front, crowding it too close for a better look.

"What the hell is 'mystical experience'?" scoffs Earwig, who had stood with his arms folded tight, refusing to join the Dancing, or turn his back on it, either one. "Olin? Don't be an idiot, okay?" His voice is urgent. "I was watching the whole time and *nothing happened*. There was no *event*." What galls him most is the emotion on display among the more awestruck and devout—the "spiritual groupies," as he calls them, "soft and runny as one-minute eggs." He derides any notion of the Dancing as "transformative," far less "a blessing" that banished "the trauma" of those first few days. Less still was it a "healing" or a "closure" of the wounds—he spits all these New Age terms with contempt. "Hey, *nothing happened*, folks, okay? That wasn't 'dancing,' for Christ sake, that was goddamn ring-around-the-rosie!" Yet even Earwig can't quite deny the shift in atmosphere, which he ascribes to barometric pressure, negative ions or whatever, the mistral or something.

Isn't it at least *conceivable*, Olin proposes to Earwig and Anders, that days of strong meditation in the cold by so many sincere pilgrims might actually generate some sort of—well, you know—*power*?

"*Power*? Oh, come on, Olin." These two very different men, the one caustic and the other antic, refuse to dignify such nonsense with debate. Yet since the Dancing, Olin has noticed, Georgie Earwig has mostly kept that savage tongue of his under control. He even joins some of the meditation periods on the selection platform, where in his determination to sit cross-legged and remain as still as "those stupid-ass Zen monks," he is rigid in infuriated agony.

TWELVE

Catherine comes down the convent path next morning as Olin is leaving for the camp. Seeing him, she smiles a little—*She must think I've lain in wait for her all night!*—and joining him, she no longer looks behind her for the other novice. It turns out that Sister Ann-Marie, in nervous collapse, has withdrawn from the retreat and will be sent for. And their chaplain (she never speaks his name) has intimated that Catherine should leave, too, since with the other novice gone, she will be "unprotected," by which, of course, he means unchaperoned.

Don't go, thinks Olin. *Just refuse to go.* Has Father Mikal any authority over her, he asks, besides the threat of a negative report?

"He is *ordained*," she says, as if this settles the matter. To question the Church's wartime entropy by seeking forgiveness from the Jews as she had done was not her place. "Poverty, chastity, obedience"—she recites these like a catechism—"*that* is my place." Is she being ironic? He cannot be sure. (Is she a virgin? The question slips furtively across his consciousness, all but unnoticed.) Her "keeper" had no choice, she says, but to report an unruly novice already on probation who won't go to him for guidance, far less Confession. And inevitably it will be decided that this disrespectful person is quite unsuitable for holy orders. "*'This one we dismiss from her novitiate,'*" she rules in stern diocesan voice. "*'She is a troublemaker. She is unworth it.'*"

"*Unworthy?*" He tries not to smile. "What nonsense."

You will have your life back! Wonderful!—that is his first reaction. He has no idea what he is talking about, yet even so, he is convinced from their discussions that this passionate young woman is too intelligent to accept the archaic strictures of the Vatican, too independent to pursue the narrow path defined for nuns by decadent male hierarchies in a corrupt structure that in the Western world, in Olin's view, is nearing the point of historical irrelevance, collapsing slowly into its own garish remains like that golden pumpkin in the autumn field.

She says nothing. In trying to comfort her and calm his heart, he talks too fast, and what he tries to say sounds irresponsible even to him. "Catherine? When you said, 'that priest'—?"

"Church business!" She is close to tears.

Retreating, he asks how she feels now about the Dancing. She looks wary, then she says, "It made me very happy." And yes, it must have been authentic: in her opinion, those who joined in with an open heart had been those most open to this whole experience of the death camp, transported by compassion to the same degree that they were truly penetrated by the horror.

She seems uneasy about walking further with him unescorted. When he moves aside to let Adina catch up and take his place, she looks relieved.

"WHY ARE YOU MESSING with her?" rasps Earwig, coming up behind. "Shame on ya." *On a so-called spiritual retreat? In fucking Ausch-witz? In a goddamn death camp?*—that's what he means, this unshaven, scowling Georgie, erstwhile scourge of nuns.

Adina, too, looks askance at his association with Catherine, and presumably Becca as well. What ails these people? Any unseemly dalliance in such a place would be unthinkable! He *knows* that, goddamnit. In no mood for rebuke, he snaps at Earwig: what makes him think this is any of his business?

The other rounds on him, enraged. "None of my business? That what you're saying, shithead?"

"You're very quick to jeer at others, I've noticed. Why are you always so pissed off? How come you don't tell us your own story?"

"*Bear my own witness*, you mean? What's that got to do with you and your little nun?" He snarls in disgust. "I never came here to bear no goddamned witness and I'm not some spiritual type like all you ecumenicals or whatever the hell you people call yourselves. You want to bear witness? Go bear witness, then. Because they haven't heard one peep out of you either. *Snotty Polack from the U.S.A., my sob story,* coming right up."

But then, abruptly, Earwig interrupts himself. "Okay, okay," he says in a low voice. "Here's all I know. The Jew list in our Romanian village was turned in to the police by the local priest, probably with Vatican approval. *These are dark times, Father, play it safe, don't get the Church in trouble.* See why I'm so hard on the Church? So these Jews got the hell downriver to Constanta on the Black Sea coast, leased an old river scow, sailed for Palestine one jump ahead of the *fascisti.*" He coughs. "Only thing, one dumb kid got left behind."

"That's you? That's terrible!"

"I was mouthy, never wrong no matter what. Must have snuck out past the pier guard, gone exploring down along the docks. I kind of remember running back, running all the way out that empty pier. '*Wait, Mama. It's me!*'" Earwig's voice has thickened oddly and his head looks skewed.

"You never seen emptiness," he says, "until you seen all that harbor water in the space where your ship should be. Darkness coming, nobody to call out to, nothing to eat, nowhere to go. And Mama out there on that ship, staring back north, maybe weeping in the dark. I see those red pinch marks yet today." He raises thumb and forefinger to the bridge of his nose. Though he lost her face over the years, he has never forgotten those marks made by cheap glasses.

"Crept into a cargo shed, whimpered all night, almost froze to death. Scared of big wharf rats. First light these Roma people came out of hiding, took me with 'em. They wanted to escape on the same ship—the *Struma*—but those nice Jews refused 'em. *Dirty Gypsies! Can't even help pay the freight unless they rob us first!* He pauses. What he can't remember was where his Roma band had wandered, which borders had been crossed, which countries. He mainly recalls being on the run after his band was arrested and a scorched summer day somewhere in eastern Europe, and a dead silent cattle car stranded on a siding, and an old belt lowered through the floor and drawn back up over and over only to be dropped and left behind in a puddle between rails when the transport jolted forward. Earwig clears his throat. "Very generous people, shared any food they could scrape up, always joked no matter what. Taught the little Jew boy how to steal," he adds. "Came in handy all my life."

"So you're here to honor them."

"Pay my respects anyway," he grumps, uncomfortable.

Olin nods. "And that's Gyorgi Earwig's story?"

"No such Jew, man. I made him up."

Earwig has no interest in going up on stage and bearing witness to that nightfall on the docks, far less what became of him after Constanta, or how he wound up in the U.S., one of thousands of refugee children, all desperate to locate their lost families. In later years, he tried to track that ship on his makeshift income as a merchant seaman, cabdriver, and part-time thief. He returned to Europe regularly, he says, and speaks five languages, all of them poorly.

Earwig's youth and middle age and all his savings have been used up in futile attempts to trace the *Struma* in the Old World ports; he found no record of that ship or her arrival in Palestine or anywhere else. As for her passengers, nothing but false leads and dead ends, like this damned place. "But coming from back of nowhere, see, with nothing to my name—no rightful name, even—it seemed like this search was all there was. Who could believe such a stupid story? What makes it even more ridiculous was not knowing the name of the people I was looking for, my own damn family. I just hoped to run across somebody who might have heard about an old Danube River scow lugging refugees to Palestine, and maybe even a young couple gone half crazy because their stupid kid got left back on the dock."

Scowling, he resumes walking. "So anyway, how can I bear witness to their story? I don't *know* their story, not how it ended.

"That guy Rainer, he's getting wartime records checked in the archives in Berlin. Same guy who dug up those name lists you people recite while you freeze your butts off out on the platform. I never stick around for that, because even if my family's name popped up, I'd never recognize it."

"Probably not," says Olin. "Certain common names take up whole columns, page after page."

"Still, I figure I must have heard it as a little kid, so maybe I would kind of *feel* it if I heard it read out loud with the right first name. Feel the good fit of it, see what I mean?" He looks embarrassed. "Don't say it, man. Even if I stumbled over the whole story, what do I do with it after all these years?" His voice is pitiless. "Who needs it? Nobody, right? Not even me."

ADINA AWAITS HIM at the cave entrance. Watching the novice passing through the tunnel, she declares without turning to look at him that "trying to undermine a devout young person's calling is a grave responsibility, whatever one's opinion of the Church. All her old doubts have been stirred awake under the influence of certain older people she respects." She eyes him coldly. "The point is, Clements, you risk doing her great harm, you and our detestable *ewige Jude*—"

"Hold on a minute, damn it! What gives you the right to lecture me like this?" For all her irritating ways, he respects Adina and her disapproval bothers him, but having watched her hover over Catherine, he has to wonder if this overbearing lady might feel possessive, even jealous.

"I just thought I should warn you," she is saying. "Catherine's intelligence and a brave spirit do not necessarily protect that girl from the sort of sophisticated older man who might stoop to the careless theft of a human heart."

"And you suspect I may be that sort of 'older man,' is that it? A stooper, so to speak?"

"Are you assuring me you're not? I'm delighted to hear that, Clements." She smiles then, warmly, hastening to mend things before he can protest further.

Well? Why should this woman trust you when you don't quite trust yourself?

Olin's brief marriage ended in divorce on grounds of what his wife's attorney cited as "alienation of the affections." In the years since, more than one lover has complained that Clements Olin can be quick to anger, remote, moody, ever ready to withdraw without offering himself fully in the first place: he is spoiled, they say, too accustomed to being courted. "Successful with women" is how his male friends might describe him, yet he feels just the reverse—he feels hollowed out by loneliness, in fact, that sense of something missing that is said to haunt his more distinguished poetry.

Although he fantasizes about remarrying, he tends to wander into passive liaisons with women already married or hopelessly enmeshed by their life dramas. One beautiful creature, said to be wasting away of a rare terminal disease, must have been misdiagnosed, he decided, since on intimate occasions, there always seemed to be plenty of her left. Another was certifiably unstable, and at least one was socially unacceptable—"quite out of the question," ruled his grandmother. He'd ignored the old lady's snobbishness, of course (or had he?), but the girl hadn't worked out anyway except in bed—the one lover, in fact, he had ever encouraged to stay with him overnight. In short, it was commonly agreed that Clements Olin was incapable of true commitment to one woman, a judgment he resisted for a time but has reluctantly come to share. Certainly he is not a man who should try to deflect a devout novice from the path of holy orders, even when convinced that she has no business on that path in the first place.

DURING THE VISIT to the Auschwitz museum on the first day, someone asked the guide why he made no mention of the murdered homosexuals. Well, they were not so many, the guide muttered. Not true, said the questioner. Speaking as a homosexual, he was outraged that even in the death camp these despised men had to wear pink triangles as badges of shame.

Last evening, a basket of pink flannel triangles had turned up by the mess hall door. This morning, at an ecumenical service on the memorial terrace, a number of people wear pink triangles under their coats. But the only ones besides the gay man and Olin who display them in full view on their parkas are young Rainer from Berlin and that earnest rabbinical student who blows the shofar. (Perhaps Sister Catherine has noticed his gesture; he takes her small nod as approval.) But when the cameraman draws near and points his camera, Olin waves him off, hoping that Catherine (who no longer stiffens when he calls her plain "Catherine") won't think him a hypocrite because of his reluctance to be recorded on film wearing that badge.

Rainer is chortling, much amused because those younger German women who are forever gushing that Herr Doktor Olin is such a gentleman, so mannerly, so handsome, are shocked by his pink badge. *Mein Gott! Him?* But these sturdy ladies are not nearly as offended as the gang of laborers tramping past on the public path across the *Lager*.

Olin wonders if he exaggerates—if he only imagines— the hostility in those stubbled lumpy faces cramped with cold. No, he does not, it's unmistakable. But what stops his heart is something he glimpsed while waving off that camera. Scanning the rows, he rediscovers the pink triangle pinned on the lapel of the black overcoat worn by Priest Mikal.

Crazy bastard! You're preaching at their church! To divert attention from the priest, he waves his fingers at the laborers, feigning good fellowship. Spotting his pink triangle, they stop short on the path, they back and fill, jeering at this homo and his motley gang of troublemaking foreigners. Inevitably Mikal's badge is spotted, too. *The new priest at the church!* Even when they move on, they continue to turn, walk backward, pointing, spitting, as the filmmaker, recording the whole episode, taunts Olin with a pantomime of those waggled fingers that, far from distracting the local men, had first drawn their attention to the priest.

THIRTEEN

Uneasy and restless throughout meditation, he soon leaves the *Lager* and, following Malan's directions, locates the winding road downriver toward the artist's deconsecrated chapel on the bluff. He has not gone far when he is hailed by Father Mikal. That he resents this priest as a threat to Sister Catherine is no excuse to hurt his feelings by being rude or cold, and even less so is the fact that Mikal may be the suspect priest mentioned by Earwig that first day on the platform. In any event, he's stuck with him and they go on together.

Father Mikal, out of shape and out of breath, says he understands that Dr. Olin had been present yesterday at the

Christian service on the platform which Sister Ann-Marie had fled; he'd be grateful for Dr. Olin's recollections of the episode and any observations he might care to make.

Perhaps he should ask the novices themselves, Olin says curtly. "I have," says the priest. Clearly his inquiry has gone nowhere and he does not care to say why. Instead, he, too, expresses reservations about Dr. Olin's "friendship" with Sister Catherine, whose spiritual guidance here is his assigned responsibility. To an impressionable young woman who has already suffered abuse on this retreat, an agnostic influence could be disturbing, he suggests, as would careless exposure to secular poetry leading to discussions of Church doctrine for which—"if you will permit me, sir?"— neither party would seem qualified.

Father Mikal, nervous and unprepossessing, with unprepossessing breath, is nonetheless civil and soft-spoken, and Olin wishes to be civil, too. He inquires brusquely how the priest happens to know so much, since he never seems to associate with his charges or attend their services. "No," says Mikal. "I am unwelcome."

"Unwelcome?"

With fingertips, the priest crosses himself minutely at the collar. "Forgive me," Olin says. "I know you can't reveal—"

"I have offered to hear Confession, you see. Give absolution. Twice. They have never come. Perhaps Sister Catherine has mentioned this?" Olin shakes his head, more and more unhappy. Like him or not, the man's isolation is painful. "But you have heard something, no doubt?" the priest insists. "Rumors, perhaps? From the convent?" It seems he's been warned by the mother superior that Sister Ann-Marie had brought malicious gossip from their diocese. "I wished to caution you, sir, that's all. For Sister Catherine's sake."

"And the good of my own soul?"

"That, too," the priest says wryly, for which Olin almost likes him.

At the bend in the river road ahead, the shuttered chapel sits stranded on its knoll. As if anticipating Olin's arrival, the old artist stands waiting in the doorway.

"Sister Catherine need not be afraid I will submit a negative report," Father Mikal says quietly, observing the old artist before turning to start back. "I won't. I admire her courage, and, if circumstances permitted, I would generally support her views." Clearly he wishes Olin to transmit this message, if only to ease Catherine's mind, and this is kind of him, Olin reflects, no matter what. Probably those convent rumors are no more than hearsay, cruel as well as false, but if so, why has this wretched Mikal gone so far out of his way to invite trouble?

"Why did you *do* that?" he calls after him, exasperated. "Wear that damn triangle, I mean," he adds when the man turns. And the priest calls back, "Perhaps because you did,

Dr. Olin. Reminding me of my duty as a Christian. And anyway, as the person who prepared those triangles, I had no choice." He seems to be trying to smile but cannot quite manage it. Setting off once more, he stumbles while blowing his nose—an uncoordinated man thrown off-balance when he tries to wave the wrong hand over his shoulder.

MALAN HAS DISAPPEARED, leaving the door open. Olin enters with a knock and trails his light step down a hallway to a whitewashed room with a bare white cloth on a wood table. Here in other days, he thinks, a silver chalice might have glittered, and candlesticks, and silver bowls.

In the vestry where he sleeps on an iron cot, the old man goes to his small stove and lights the gas under his kettle. "I feared you'd bring him in here," he says shortly, retrieving a used tea bag and two chipped cups and saucers from the shelf above.

"You know him, then?"

"By reputation."

But the old artist has no real interest in Mikal or his reputation and says no more. In setting his table, pouring the tea, he extends a bony wrist on which Olin can see (as he is meant to, he suspects; pride of precedence exists even in Hell) the faded blue number with three digits only that identifies the bearer as one of the earliest prisoners in Auschwitz. "Five years," Malan says softly; he weighed less than a starved dog, he says, when he was freed.

Olin's Polish friends knew Malan in the postwar years in Warsaw. In all those years, they say, he made no mention of the death camp: in some way, his unconscious sealed it off like the secret garret confining the wild bastard child or the mad brother. He was already elderly when a stroke set free his memory, and soon thereafter, like the escaped prisoner, Stanislav K., drawn by a longing he cannot explain, this fragile old man forsook the security of his family and returned to the vicinity of the dead *Lager*, envisioning a final work that might liberate him from its grasp before he died.

A kind of homesickness, both old men had called it—was that a clue? But if so, clue to what, precisely? What constitutes home?

He follows his host by lantern light down a steep ladder: his fingertips, extended for balance, rake a strange silk off spider-webbed stones. An earth-floored basement of four or five small chambers has the dank smell of a cave: from floor to ceiling on white-plastered walls, winding through the doorless rooms like a huge headless caterpillar, decapitated yet still probing, still seeking escape, this black-and-white mural with no beginning and no end is a pure hallucination of fragmented images and symbols across which hole-eyed specters drift in eternal nightmare.

"My God," says Olin. Here they are, he thinks, all the hungry ghosts, the silenced voices, not descending from the heavens but arising from the dark.

Freshly astonished by his own creation, Malan makes no effort to explain it. "You can always read about the camp," the old man whispers. "My pictures avoid showing the camp but it is everywhere in them all the same. It is in me." Art, he believes—not art appreciation but the creation of it—is the one path that might lead toward apprehension of that ultimate evil beyond all understanding. "The hand can speak when words cannot," he adds. "The only way to understand such evil is to reimagine it. And the only way to reimagine it is through art, as Goya knew. You cannot portray it realistically."

The old man is grateful he feels strong enough to complete this vast creation that was sealed up inside him for so long; he only hopes it might fulfill a promise made to fellow prisoners, to record the horror of their suffering should he survive.

"I'll die in peace, you see," he murmurs happily, waving his cane as if to banish all those hole-eyed ghosts at last. He cares not at all that so few will see his masterpiece, which in any case will only last until the day this old chapel entombs it by crumbling into its cellar. Meanwhile, he suggests, local schoolchildren might be led down his ladder and a few at least might learn and understand.

Olin nods politely but says nothing. Sensing his guest's skepticism, Malan falls silent. "No, I suppose not," he says after a pause. Escorting Olin to the door, he changes the subject. "In Cracow," he says, "you might wish to visit the old Franciscan cathedral and have a look at its modern stained-glass window. You'll find something very interesting, I think."

"What sort of thing?"

Malan ignores that question. He is astonished that foreigners would come from far away to sit in silence in the great dead ruin at Birkenau. "And what do you think about all day, out there alone?" he inquires shyly, pointing at the tower in the distance.

ACCORDING TO OLIN'S research notes, Tadeusz Borowski's postwar years were spent in refugee camps and solitary wanderings: in a letter from Paris, he described himself as "a visitor from a dead, detested country." But some of his stories and poems were being published, and in this period he would locate his Maria, now a war refugee in Sweden; eventually they would reunite and marry. In 1948, when his death camp narrative made him famous, he was twenty-five years old.

That same year, he returned to Poland, joined the Communist Party, and became its virulent propagandist, and in this period, he made a "special mission" to Berlin for the satellite government—apparently successful, since he was soon assigned another. Borowski never talked about these "missions": was he ashamed of them, Olin wondered? A friend who years earlier had been tortured by the Gestapo for crimes against the state was now being tortured by Polish security on a like charge, presumably to extract a confession before the show trial at which Borowski was scheduled to testify: did he fear he might be coerced to malign his friend by the threat of torture or return to prison?

In the last year of his life, he told a friend that in regard to his literary gifts, he might as well have laid a shovel handle across his own bared throat and stood on it (a favored *Kapo* method of extinguishing fallen slaves too weak to work).

Which Borowski was it, then—the corrupted, cynical Vorarbeiter Tadeusz of the death camp stories or the real-life "Tadek" who (according to his fellow poet Czeslaw Milosz) had behaved well in the camps? Which man sank onto his knees in July 1951 as if to puke into the toilet and stuck his head into the oven and turned on the gas, ladies and gentlemen, at twenty-eight years of age, just three days after the birth of his first child, a baby daughter, unable to live his life even one more day?

Why? Because he had betrayed his great gifts as a writer? Because toward the end he had betrayed his wife and longtime lover by succumbing to an affair with a young girl? Because he feared that to save himself he might be forced to betray—or had already betrayed—his imprisoned friend? Or because as a lifelong idealist, he was fatally depressed by the realization that Europe—mankind—had learned nothing from years of suffering, and nothing had changed?

> *In this war morality . . . the ideals of freedom,*
> *justice, and human dignity had all slid off man*
> *like a rotten rag. We said there is no crime that a*
> *man will not commit in order to save himself.*
> *And, having saved himself, he will commit*
> *crimes for increasingly trivial reasons . . . first*
> *out of duty, then from habit, and finally—for*
> *pleasure.*

In suicide, Borowski had borne witness, too.

TOWARD DUSK, headed back along the platform toward the Gate, Olin discovers the outline of the mutilated cross under light snow. Two days earlier, he had lingered only long enough to kick at the gouged gravel with his boot toe. Today he is determined to scrape and smooth that cross as a gift to Catherine, and looks for that plywood shard that Sister Ann-Marie had tossed aside. But her implement is lost under blowing snow, and in the end he reaches down and tries to blur the scar with swipes of his gloved hand. However, the compacted gravel is still frozen, and finally he gives up and straightens, arching his back. Then, with a curse, he drops onto his knees and rakes at the rough cross with numb clawed fingers. In the end, it relents and is mostly leveled but not before his gloves are worn through and his fingertips are scraped and bleeding, stuck with black gravel; in the cold air, they sting when he tries to brush them off. "Bloody hell," he whispers. He gets to his feet and walks on toward the tunnel, his sore hands shoved into his parka.

The others have all gone but she is there. "I saw," she says. "The wound." She takes his torn forefingers in her hand and with her handkerchief, not gently, dabs away the crust of blood and gravel.

"I saw," she repeats, still holding his fingers. "He *kneeled*. Before the *Cross*." She rolls her eyes heavenward, looking comically devout. "O Lord, bless this good man who prays."

"No prayers today, miss. Sorry."

"*Sorry, miss*, he says!" She opens her eyes wide in wonder. Still mocking her own piety, she raises her hands high, palms pressed together, as if in gratitude for such a miracle. "He *kneeled!* Alone in wind and snow!"

Emerging from the tunnel, they walk in silence down the frozen road, the only sound the light tick of their shoes. Maintaining her space, she hops across the frozen ruts rather than take his elbow. But at a certain moment—and both feel it when it comes—they turn slowly as they walk and look each other frankly in the face for the first time, look away at once, then look right back and this time hold, still walking.

"Who are you, then?" she murmurs. *Are your eyes telling the truth?* Is that what she means? *Are you only playing games? And if so, why?* Because in this terminus, in the very shadow of that gate, a feckless dalliance would be beyond all shame.

"I don't know," he says as they move onward. And her nod assures him she has faith that he is doing his utmost to be truthful.

Over and over, with no need of further speech or signal, they drift apart as on a transparent tether, snap back in place quick as two quick fishes.

Look at you, grinning your fool head off! You happy or what? "I'll going to miss you, Catherine," says this happy man, but his intensity of feeling makes it seem that what he confesses in this moment is, "I love you."

Instant doubt: is that his happiness reflected in her eyes?

Can this rare creature be anywhere near where he is in his heart? If so, what can she be thinking? How can she behave as if this moment weren't extraordinary, as if this road were just any old dirt road in Poland, leading from this point to that one, here to there?

And that vision of Emi in her dying—had that, too, been delusion? And his queer homesickness? He struggles to think clearly. Perhaps Catherine will assume he's teasing her again, playing the romantic idiot, the old fool. And, under the circumstances, it might be best for all concerned if she believes that.

In his confused state, the light sound of their steps on the frozen road is the sole reality.

WHERE THE ROAD disappears under asphalt at the edge of town, he hangs back a bit, to give her space to arrive unaccompanied. Understanding his tact, she does not slow nor does she look back. Only once do they exchange a glance of scared bewilderment—*Did that really happen? If so, what was it?*—before she hurries off to vespers in the convent.

Olin's edginess, watching her go, is caught by Earwig, who spits elaborately as he walks past. Well? Whose business is it that two mismatched people have made friends? Or even stumbled into an attraction? Leading an unworldly young woman astray would certainly be disgraceful were he playing games. He's not! True, he'd gone too far with that silly spasm of affection on the road, but it's hardly as though he'd compromised her with a vow of undying love. And yet, with only one day left, he already misses her so badly that after supper he stalks the cobbled courtyard, awaiting her arrival for the evening meeting. However, it is not Catherine who appears out of the dark but Stefan, who looks displeased to be seen coming from the convent. "Aha," he says, as if Olin's presence here has cleared up a mystery. "You're waiting for her, I suppose."

"You've known Sister Catherine for some time, it seems," Olin says carefully.

"Amalia? Indeed I have." He and "Amalia" were "old comrades" in the reform movement in their diocese. Her convent was no great distance from his seminary, Stefan is saying. They met in a group of progressive students.

"You submitted some sort of reform petition, right? And she supported you?"

Well, she signed his petition. And there were other circumstances, he adds, with a certain coyness that Olin dislikes very much. Which other circumstances? What is this man intimating here? Why is he so often nearby when Catherine is present, and never averts that impertinent bald stare when Olin stares back, to challenge him, but only smiles in the same knowing way he is smiling now?

These days, Amalia (Stefan says), disillusioned with the secular world, longs for the purity of her original commitment, of that cloistered life for which she is temperamentally so unsuited. He has always tried to educate her about all the scandals and cover-ups in Rome, he says, but she will no longer let him near for fear he might contaminate her fragile faith.

Stefan has pitched his voice louder, apparently intending this last supposition to be overheard by Sister Catherine, who now approaches down the convent path. "She thinks I'm some anti-papist fanatic maligning the Mother Church. The difference is that unlike your Jew friend, I know what I'm talking about. From the inside."

"Unlike my Jew friend," Olin says. "I see."

Catherine has stopped. "What is it you want, Stefan?" she inquires in a low tense voice—less a question than a warning. The ex-monk winks at Olin and retreats inside.

Neither coldly nor warmly, she awaits him. "What has he been telling you, Mr. Olin?"

"Oh, only that you two worked together as young students. Flirted a little, maybe?" he suggests perversely. "I mean, that's not so serious, young people flirting—"

"No flirts!"

Cut off so sharply, he suffers a disagreeable foreboding,

undefined and fleeting. With all her heart she had supported that petition, she is saying, feeling sorry for an idealistic young monk who had entrusted her with his life story. Only afterward had she suspected that much of his life story might be untrue.

Afterward? A liaison, then? The prude in him recoils from the image of that sallow monk possessing this warm young body standing so close at this moment to his own. Sensing something of his turmoil, she is flushing, too.

"I don't mean to upset you, Catherine. I'm just teasing. As I told you this afternoon, I'm going to miss you very much, remember? Probably you thought I was just being silly." He looks past those intent green eyes so as not to see it, should she happen to agree.

"Silly," she repeats, tasting the word. His attempt to modify his avowal by making it sound somehow facetious has confused her, she is searching his expression for the joke. Evidently deciding he has been fooling all along, she musters a thin smile before proceeding indoors, and he has no choice but to smile with her; his fervent avowal of this afternoon has been reduced to banter.

With everything so unresolved, his lungs sag under the weight of tomorrow's parting. He has been deluded even by himself, he sees that now. Among other things, he has never wished to recognize his unseemly attraction to the young female form hiding naked as a nut within the husk of her

dull clothing. An unaccountable, in fact unthinkable, attraction, he would have said only two days ago, since quite
apart from being sacrosanct, untouchable, she had looked
so frumpy with that hacked-off hair, not his sort of woman
at all.

FOURTEEN

Approaching the auditorium, Olin is pulled aside by Erna, who leads him back outside into the courtyard: the woman can't stop hunting! Erna has sniffed out somebody's uncle whose elderly brother-in-law, a longtime patient of Dr. Allgeier who later took work as a camp guard, recognized Madame Allgeier and her daughters on the selection platform in late 1942; he risked execution by the SS, he claims, for trying to slip them his lunch sandwich for old times' sake. In fifty years, he has never forgotten how the young schoolteacher had urged him to go feed his damned sandwich to that other collaborator polluting her father's house. "Looks like our little Jew girl hurt his feelings on her way to the cremo," Erna grins. "She must have been a fighter, Baron. Not like you."

❦

FOLLOWING CATHERINE through the door of the auditorium, he cannot see her face, which spares him the disillusioned look he fears. "As Adina keeps reminding me," he whispers hoarsely from behind, "I'm old enough to be your father. 'No fool like an old fool,' right?" This angling for reassurance is contemptible: he could bite his tongue off. In his insecurity he has banished a spell, and their dance of spirits on the road this afternoon—if it had any reality at all—must be gone forever, just as he discovers how dear to him she has become.

❦

CATHERINE TAKES THE SEAT beside Adina Schreier. Unnerved, he does not join them. Rainer waves and so he moves in that direction. Unlike the Poles, the Germans are well-scattered, giving up comfort in numbers to avoid any appearance of defiant solidarity. Mercifully, most of the retreatants are well-meaning and are taking pains not to isolate these people, but the tension dispelled by the Dancing has been seeping back. In this toxic atmosphere, good intentions are eroding like the noses of stone gargoyles on cathedral peaks.

As he approaches, Rainer makes a place for him, but he does not stop moving, he must *act*, and in moments, he finds himself impelled onto the stage as if snatched there by a puppet master and set down on dangling limp legs behind the podium. Not at all sure what he needs to say, he gapes at the startled faces of Catherine and Adina in the second row.

He nods, coughs, clears his throat, and finally sets forth, taking refuge in the judicious manner of D. Clements Olin, Ph.D., embarked upon a formal lecture at his university. Surely we can all agree, he huffs, that Nazi Germany carried cold genocide further than any regime in this genocidal century, noisily supported, he puffs, by that rabble of Jew-haters who sprang forth like weeds not only here in Poland but in every one of the twelve countries represented in this audience this evening, his own included.

Though obvious, this indictment grabs attention, and in the quiet, in a quiet voice, he challenges any person present—French, Dutch, British, Belgian, Spanish, Swiss, American, no matter—to raise a hand who can honestly claim that his own nation's history remains unstained in this regard.

Chairs budge loudly and heavy muttering pervades the room but no hand rises.

All nations, he continues, and all religions, cultures, and societies throughout history have perpetrated massacres, large and small: man has been a murderer forever. A dangerous animal tragically unbalanced by its own intelligence and predisposed to violence—

"Hear, hear!" calls Dr. Anders Stern, endorsing his own oft-reiterated point even while warning his esteemed colleague Dr. Olin that, however excellent his discourse, he'd better get on with it or risk losing his audience. Already somebody is calling, "Nobody came to this damned place to listen to a speech." And another voice: "We're here to bear witness, right? Tell your own story."

"Why are you trying to hide the Germans behind generalizations about human behavior?" a third voice inquires. "How can you morally equate gangs of fascist killers with millions of innocent martyrs? Compared to European Jews, you Americans know *nothing* about anti-Semitism! You're not even a Jew!"

In the doorway stands Erna, bare arms folded. Has she understood what that last voice had said? Will she contradict it? Will she expose him? Because other than Erna there are no witnesses, no records. The last few elders who might cobble up the truth will never have occasion to recall dead rumors and lost names of long ago.

He can return to the U.S. and resume his former identity as the historian and poet Clements Olin, isn't that true?

Years before, half-listening to his car radio, he'd been assailed by a voice as aggravating as the pinpoint racket of the small hard-shelled insect that whirred its way one summer day into his inner ear; what had maddened him was the quasi-British accent he'd been trying to eradicate since those years after the war, when he'd been shipped abroad for schooling. What it was, in fact, was his own recorded voice, reciting his poetry. He hears that disembodied voice say now, as if speaking from afar, "You are mistaken, sir. I speak as a Polish Jew."

In the hush, Adina's face jumps forth from the second row like a pale balloon. Catherine, beside her, is nodding to herself, eyes closed, as if to say, *Oh Lord, I think I knew.*

Suppressing the truth a moment longer might have choked him: to feel clear again, all of a piece, he has to spit it out or give up breathing. But having done so while still not sure he has the courage of it, he must now fight down an impulse to retreat or at least explain why he has said nothing before now.

He informs the audience that he comes from an old Protestant family of this region which had fled to America just prior to the war, leaving his father's pregnant fiancée behind. Born in Cracow, he'd been ransomed as an infant and baptized Clements soon after his arrival in the U.S. His mother vanished, and after that, his questions about her were stifled—out of deference to his father's grief, he was always told. "I was strongly encouraged to forget her. But here in Poland, with kind local assistance"—he indicates the formidable Erna, who stands in the doorway, bare arms still folded, looking not kindly in the least—"some inquiries have been made." Gasping, he must pause to find his breath. "And we have confirmed that her maternal ancestry was probably Jewish."

"*Probably* Jewish?" somebody jeers: it's Jaroslav, Becca's sarcastic lover. "Are you suggesting she was 'not quite Jewish'? Does that mean you're not quite Jewish either?"

Ignoring Jaroslav, he says, "I believe today that from the beginning the Olinskis had little doubt about what became of her. And yes, perhaps, deep in my heart, I knew it, too." He'd fled the confirmation of her fate far longer than he'd let himself believe: he's had to face that fact, he says, since he arrived here. That his family lost track of Emmeline Allgeier, that's one thing. People disappear in wartime. What he cannot forgive is that even *after* the Cold War, no one went looking for her. Was that because, if no trace of her ever turned up, there would be no evidence that his mother had perished in the camps, therefore no proof of Jewish blood in their precious lineage? Because that, he says, was almost certainly their main concern.

LEAVING THE STAGE, he avoids looking at Catherine. The Germans try to engage him with wan smiles but his Polish friends shift in their seats, look past his head, peer at their hands when he sits down nearby. At the intermission they rise and file outside for a smoke; having already decided (he assumes) that this damned American has been deceiving them, they will simply exclude him. Bumping past his knees, Zygmunt grumbles, scarcely looking at him, "So, then, Clements, you bear a little witness after all?"— sarcasm, not a real question, and well short of an invitation to rejoin them.

Sitting solitary in his row can only draw attention. He is already rising when shrewd Anders in the row behind says, "Come on, Jew-boy, let's get it over with." Taking Olin's elbow as if he were infirm, the boisterous Swede with the loopy grin steers him outside and loiters nearby in case support is needed. In a moment, Earwig shows up, too.

The Poles finish their cigarettes before turning to acknowledge him. Only Rebecca smiles, taking his hand. "So, Baron, you are not too proud to be a poor Jew like me?" She might be the only one in this glum bunch, he thinks, with any play in her.

"I've only been one for a few minutes, Becca. I don't know yet."

The others listen, unamused. "Not that it matters in the least, dear Clements," Nadia murmurs, resting her hand a moment on his forearm. "That ugly hate is finished in our country now. We are all friends, are we not, my Becca?" With a quick vixen show of teeth, she flashes a fake smile and Becca flashes one right back: both women laugh.

"The hating? It's all finished, you say, Nadia?" As usual, dour Jaroslav has missed the joke. "Among our so-called intelligentsia, perhaps."

Zygmunt is intent on Olin's face. "No, excuse me, Clements, I do not believe it. You just don't look like them, I'm sorry."

"Them?" says Becca, and Nadia protests, "Oh Zyg, *really*! Remember those blue-eyed ones we saw in Ukraine?"

Disliking all Poles on general principles, Earwig won't waste this fine chance to offend them. "Any Pole who calls himself a man," he growls, "would take this dirty Jew outside and shoot him."

Anders hoots. "Shoot him? Hurrah! I say so, too! I have seen this Hebrew naked in our room!" Though he has seen no such thing, he points a damning finger at Olin's crotch. "Circumcised, my friends. Utterly he is circumcised, this unfortunate Jewish! Better you shoot him!"

Amused at first, the Poles are quick to take offense at the implied insult from this wacky Swede. Nadia tucks away her smile. "Clements? Did I hear you call yourself a 'Polish Jew'?" She is intent on this. "Because there's really no such thing."

"Maybe your people lived abroad too long? Forgot how all this worked back in the old country?"

"Forgot how *what* worked, Jaro? My father was Polish, my mother apparently part-Jewish. Why doesn't that make me a Polish Jew?"

"Apparently?" That sarcasm again. "Tell me, Baron, will the Polish part hang on to the patronymic?"

"As a Jew, I suppose you mean. I'll let you know."

"If your mama was Jewish, you are, too," says Becca, taking his arm. "But our dear Nadia, this good, kind-hearted Nadia, she is correct also. Even here in our brave new democracy, one is a Jew or one is Polish, never both, not really. New laws may say different but all Poles know this in their guts. You understand this, Clements? Jews in Germany liked to imagine they were Germans—'German Jews.' No Jew in Poland made that mistake."

Becca's tone has tightened. "So yes I am Jewish, and also I am Polish, but even among these good dear friends I do not call myself a 'Polish Jew.' What you have here, Baron, is Polish intelligentsia befriending their pet Jewess."

Stung by her bitterness, her friends look exasperated and unhappy, but nobody dares contradict her. She is too volatile, he thinks, too smart. Too fucking dangerous.

When her companions return inside, Becca hangs back in the doorway. "Is it true, Clements? Your *schlachta* family never wished to know what had become of her?" Her tone is gentle but relentless. "But she is the real reason why you came here, yes? Or the reason you stayed away?"

"Probably both," he says.

Nadia has overheard. "You say she died here? In this *Lager*?" All turn to look at him. *Why didn't you tell us*, their expressions say. "It appears so," he says shortly.

"Come on, Jaro!" Kind Becca is changing the subject, pointing toward the podium. "If our new Jew here can bear witness, why not you?" Jaroslav snaps back meanly, telling her to mind her own damned business. Abruptly, then, he rises. Though welcomed by Ben Lama, he does not go forward; he intends to make this quick. Eyes cast down, he mumbles all but inaudibly ("Speak up!") in one short burst about the race dissension and dissolution that all but destroyed his family in that ugly war. "For them, maybe tragedy would be better," he says, then sits down as suddenly as he had risen. "Like a jack-in-a-box!" laughs Becca. But she takes Jaro's hand when she sees how he is trembling and is unoffended when he snatches it away.

HE OVERTAKES CATHERINE as she leaves the building. Just as he feared, she stiffens when he touches her arm, pausing only to see what he might want. He has something to show her, he says. They perch on the cold edge of the stone bench in the court, where he brings out his precious photo. "This girl was my mother, you see," he explains senselessly. Hoarse, he clears his throat and blunders on. "I didn't want to exploit her story just to dramatize my own."

She regards him with bewilderment. Was he ashamed of her?

Oh Lord, she's missing the whole point. No, no, of course not, he protests, why should he feel ashamed? He had only hoped to avoid unnecessary drama until he could be certain of the facts. *Not true. The facts were no longer in question, only your willingness to live with them.*

She sits silent, awaiting some sign that she is free to go. He tries to smile but his mouth is dry, he has to swallow. "I suppose you see me a bit differently now? Perhaps like me a bit less?" He intends this wryly but hears fear in it, knowing she will hear it, too.

"Like you less?" She is too unpracticed in mendacity and tact not to hunt out ambiguity, club it to death. "Can it be you who likes you less?"

His nod concedes this: yes, that's possible. (They had seemed so close only hours ago, why can't she simply scoff away his distress?)

"Catherine? May I? Is it all right, I mean, to call you Catherine?" *Pathetic! Unbelievable! You've been calling her Catherine for two days!*

"It is all right," she sighs, looking mystified.

In desperation, he invokes their bond on that walk this afternoon, that exaltation. "You felt it, too, I think." She nods. "And also in the Dancing?" She nods again, looking unhappy. *What a pity to speak of it*, she must be thinking. *You only smear the colors.* "So anyway," he concludes stiffly, sitting back, desperate to recoup a little dignity, "I do think it's important that we stay in touch after we leave here."

She reminds him that this will not be possible, there can be no such prospect. But then she whispers, "You say to me that you will miss me. I say to you I miss you now this minute."

Oh my God. His start of joy gives way at once to alarm. He takes her hand, searches her face to be sure of what she means. What if she's serious? What happens now? Has he cornered her, coerced her into this avowal to cushion his damned ego? How does he handle this? How does he protect her from her own impulsiveness? Protect her from herself?

Gently removing her hand from his, she crosses herself. "Yes," she whispers. "The Lord has willed that this sister of Christ and this good man, her Jew brother, should meet here on Golgotha." She touches cool fingertips to his brow in simple blessing.

"Ah." He nods as best he can with the wind knocked out of him. Her blessing had been no more than Christian mercy, the sealing of some covenant or other.

But—*I miss you now this minute?* Hadn't she said that, too? Could she be so fearful of the consequences that she has hidden her true feelings from herself, just as he had? Or is she the mature one, the wiser head prevailing, the first to awaken from that dreaming walk of yesterday and look hard at the impossibility of their situation?

The story of his life, continued: the impracticality of

serious commitment to one woman, yet again. *Dr. Clements Olin, Jew brother of New England, wishes to announce his unrequited love for the comely novice Sister Catherine . . .*

How right they were, his friends. How he regrets—how he *detests*—his foolish attendance on this much younger person in the role of mentor, taking advantage of her hunger for poetry and cultural ideas in a low effort to impress her and engage her affections, all the while nursing a lecherous curiosity about the live young body under those dead clothes.

He struggles to speak, to say anything at all that might salvage the moment or at least get it behind them, but she raises her forefinger to her lips as to a child, hushing further foolish speech. The tears welling in her eyes will never fall. She says, "We—everyone, I mean—I think what we are feeling in this place is much too large for one simple soul to understand, too powerful." That transcendence of yesterday along the road from Birkenau, she agrees fervently, was like the Dancing, overflowing from some source they cannot know. "And this feeling of love overflowing is so strong that we become confused, perhaps take it for something else—"

"Something sentimental? We risk romanticizing the whole experience, I suppose you mean." He wants to sound casual, to let go gracefully, but surely his cracked voice betrays him.

She waves a pale hand at the surrounding dark. "And still they are singing in me, Mr. Olin. In you also?"

Singing in me? "I suppose so, Catherine." He is thinking of Malan's hole-eyed specters.

Leading them back onto safe ground, she tells him how grateful she was that he spoke out in defense of the German "friends." However, he must look stricken still, for she touches his hand in concern. "Mr. Olin? How are you feeling now?"

He is taken aback by her tenderness. "I do wish you'd call me Clements," he invites her, wishing he hadn't, knowing she won't. Gruffly, he tells her he feels fine, tells her again how moved he'd been by her brave words at the ash pond, all the while aware that he is blithering like any idiot, twining himself in lies and contradictions.

She rises to go. He jumps up, too, fishing the autumn-colored amber from his pocket and pressing it into her hand. "A keepsake. Please. So you won't forget all our good talks, I mean. Our walks along that road."

She draws back in alarm, as Wanda had. "Please, Mr. Olin, no, I cannot accept!" But to his astonishment, tears are coming that she cannot hide, and it is now when her face curls and she is pitiful and plain that he knows how precious to him she has become.

"Catherine, listen," he whispers. "You fear a negative report, isn't that true? But Father Mikal assured me—"

"How can they refuse me?" she bursts out. "It is my calling." Like St. Catherine, she had offered her life to the good Lord, not to those old red-robed men in Rome. Who, she says, would entrust the sacred gift of this one life on earth to a hierarchy of usurpers unworthy of respect? If necessary, she declares fiercely, she will ordain *herself*, live a devout life outside the convent walls, join the great emancipation of the nuns that must surely come! Go forth into the world with the Lord's blessing and drive the last false priests out of the temples—!

But as she withdraws toward the convent, she looks frightened by her own bravado. "Everything will be all right," he calls after her stupidly, full of emotion, and then— stupider still—"Don't worry, Catherine, you'll see. I shall take care of you."

"Take care of me?" She crosses herself, incredulous. "By no means will that be necessary!" She is gone before he can undo the damage.

HE MOUNTS THE STAIRS slowly to the dormitory floor, goes to the naked washroom to piss out his chagrin. In the rust-pocked mirror over the stained basin, he derides the spurned suitor who washes his hands of himself in vain and must shake the water off and dry his hands down his trouser seams like a little boy for want of a coarse paper towel. Never has he felt so clumsy, so inept, so immature. The face in the mirror fairly glowers in self-detestation.

Who are you anyway, some kind of a dumb Polack? Some weird kind of a Jew? Merely an idiot? Whatever made you think your ridiculous infatuation was reciprocated in the smallest way? She's been trying all along to tell you gently that the last thing she needs right now is some old fool blundering into her life and causing trouble.

He harangues his mirror image as he had so often in his first years at university, usually drunk and not infrequently ashamed of some callow utterance or unkind act of the previous hour that he hadn't been quite ready to face up to.

⁂

HAD EITHER GRANDPARENT EVER KISSED or hugged him? He could scarcely recall their touch except to slap or shake him, and that rarely, since as a shy and lonely child, he had been disobedient only through confusion. Not that he'd missed being pecked by thin cold lips or embraced by the bony arms of those old stalks with their queer odors— in fact, the idea repelled him. But his father hadn't been much good at affection either, and he supposed he had longed for something always missing—indeed, ached for it—if only perhaps a hug when he was sad, or at least some sense that he belonged with a group of human beings whose affection might help fill that empty pit at the bottom of every breath he'd ever taken.

And now his life is all too much and much too suddenly a shambles. Today he is a Jew who knows next to nothing about being Jewish. How ironic, no, how *grotesque* it would be if even now he remained infected with some old strain of anti-Semitism contracted from those snobs who raised him, having discovered too late that in this last of the Olinskis, they were fostering some damned bastardly little Jew. How bitterly they must have resented him, this ill-begotten David, seed and symbol of their disappointment in a drunkard son.

Still, they had done their duty by him. As they saw it, sparing him the rumor of his provenance had been a kindness. Had his father been braver and more truthful, of course, they might never have ransomed some little smeller they had never laid eyes on. Sound arguments against it would surely have been found. The paternity, indeed the very existence of this "David" might have been disputed, in which case he would have perished with Miss Emi Allgeier in the last burning gasp of an earthly passage too fleeting and too terrible to count as life at all.

Emmeline Allgeier? You came looking for her, yes, if tell-

ing yourself so makes you feel better. But how clearly did you understand that was why you came? And did you really wish to find her? Wish to learn that laughing Emi in the window was gone and lost forever in the wastes of history, along with every soul who ever knew her voice or took delight in her or might have mourned her?

Her only mourner is this whiner in the mirror. *That you, David? Welcome to bloody Poland, man. This was your decision, you whose heart fastened on that instinct that something awaited you in the "dead, detested country" of old* Vorarbeiter. *Well, now you know, right? So make the best of it.*

True, he would never have chosen to be Jewish, to declare publicly, I am a Jew. He doesn't feel it. Must he feel it? Only a masochist would reassign himself to an alienated group that even in the U.S. may sometimes be subjected to subtle or covert exclusion. *Is it really so shameful to avoid being excluded? To avoid being . . . well, stigmatized? Isn't that the word you're dodging? (Can you tell us, sir, just why you feel that being Jewish is a stigma?)*

You don't have to be David, remember? If you can't handle it, it's not too late to turn your back on the whole business. Just go home and shut up.

In the mirror, the shadow of a smile, a very small one. And he says aloud, "You're just a poor old Jew now, Baron. And you do have to be David, like it or not."

The only whole heart is the broken heart, but it must be wholly broken, wasn't that what the rabbi told them? That more breakage may be awaiting him he does not doubt. It's right there in those eyes in the mirror. He can see it.

IN THE BAD LIGHT in his room, Olin can scarcely write his notes and anyway, still madly restless, he is sick to death of words.

A shout on the stair, a senseless banging, then a gleeful Rainer in the doorway. Those two florid ladies from München who adore the handsome and distinguished Herr Doktor Professor Olin? And had been so shocked when the Herr Doktor Professor wore that horrible pink triangle at Birkenau? Well, imagine their dismay upon hearing his confession earlier this evening! "First ting, filty perfert iss!" protests Anders in his idea of comic German, clapping his hands over his ears, "*Und* den, next ting, *ein Jude!*"

Rainer laughs loudly, Anders, too. When Olin barely smiles, Rainer retreats down the stair. But this damned Swede won't let it go, he will beat this joke into submission or know the reason why.

As Olin turns off the weak light, Anders parodies the traditional drinking song in which the singer bids adieu to his companions. "A Jew, a Jew, kind friends, a Jew (Ja, ja, a Jew!). I can't no longer shtay mit you (Shtay mit you!). *Ja, ja,* dey hank mein hardt from a veeping villow tree, und der vorld don't hurt no more from me . . ." Here the Nordic Jew runs out of lyric and invention and his song dies when in the dark his roommate does not stir or make a sound.

⁂

IN DREAM, Olin wanders the haunted corridors of the night barracks. In his hand like a token of admission is his photo. Is her face the one he seeks among those pale bald creatures looming off the walls? The shorn heads can't console him, and the missing one is nowhere to be found. *Mama?* he calls. *Mama? No butterflies live here, Mama!* And from the black tarn of his dream, a child's voice whispers, very near, *Oh Mama, you never even knew how much I missed you.*

IN PARADISE

FIFTEEN

In the early morning of the day of departure—the bus will leave for Cracow at midday—he sets out alone toward Birkenau under a shifting sky withholding snow. Soon it is snowing, and the cold whiteness encloses him in the snow silence. Early in life, if only in the womb, he might even have traveled this mud-rutted road where on this morning a half century later his boots strike his native earth. This road with its shoulder of hard-pruned trees is the road he feels fated to travel to some final destination. *Heimgang*—the peculiar word hangs in his consciousness— is that a German word? These Germans have denied it, looking puzzled, yet in his poor brain it has an intimation that no other word seems to convey. Homegoing? The way home? It has fate in it, and that elusive homesickness.

Figures scattered down the road behind neither catch

up nor drift back to await company, having no more wish than he does, it appears, to call out to others and thereby dispel this unnamable odd longing that has drawn them to walk this road alone on this last morning.

From down the platform, he glances back as the figures emerge singly from the tunnel and his heart jumps because Catherine is there, her blue beret passing through the fence into the women's compound. Has she seen him? Next time he turns, she's gone.

At Crematorium #2, heart-shaped prints of a small deer traverse new snow on the tilted slabs of collapsed concrete from beneath which—how many days ago?—those icy emanations had seeped forth to chill his soul. Precariously, dislodging rotting bricks, he climbs down into a corner of the cellar. In a crevice of the poisoned chamber small winter-bitten mosses and pale fungi and sparse lichens have established life.

Here he chips out a niche and painstakingly inters his Polish amber, entreating Emi to forgive him this small offering already refused by others after taking all these years to come find her.

AT THE GATE, he gazes all about about him one last time. The day is not far off, he supposes, when commercial interests will protest that these old pasturelands, having outlived their usefulness as an exhibit of the state museum, are a shocking waste of real estate and taxes. The last barracks, the last guard post, all that barbed wire and broken brick, will be stripped off and scavenged. The spring woods and high picket fences will soften if not quite conceal the naked slabs of those indecent ruins and in time the weather will transform the ash pits into lily ponds, and broad fresh meadows will be suitable once more for butterflies, wildflowers, children's voices, Sunday strolling, picnics, trysts, walked dogs, escaped balloons, and all manner of municipal occasions. Even its picturesque old name, Brzezinka, can only enhance the marketing potential of the grand development to follow. Birchwood Estates? The Birches? Birch Tree Meadows?

THEY ARE EMBARRASSED by a last encounter in the courtyard. Almost shyly, he invites her to join him on a visit to the Leonardo portrait in Cracow: if the museum is closed by the time they arrive this afternoon, they can go there first thing in the morning. "If novices still wore wimples, you would look a bit like her," he suggests, producing his postcard of Cecilia.

She inspects the card politely, starts to frown when he

watches too intently. Returning it, she whispers, "Please, do not look at me that way."

For a few seconds, taking back the postcard, he holds on to those slim fingers. Should he ever return to Poland, he is saying, he would be so happy to come see her—

She is trying hard to smile and free her fingers. *"Don't!"* she commands him. He lets go. She has escaped whatever hold he had on her and does not wish to slip back, lose her footing—that's how he reads this. And in his hunger to hold her, hug her to his breast to ease all this constriction in his heart, he actually emits a little yelp of pain. So ridiculous is this that he tries to smile but can't manage that either. "I meant it, Catherine," he says quietly. "I would have liked that very much."

"I, too!" she cries, wide-eyed, thrusting the words at him, much as she'd thrust her diary that first day, and he senses something coming he won't care to hear. It's no business of his, he tells her hastily, there's no need to entrust him with a confidence.

With a groan, she raises her palms to her cheekbones, peers at him between her fingers: it is all too much for her. "Everyone trusts Dr. Olin except Dr. Olin," she whispers. And then she flees, as if remembering some urgent task that must be seen to before the bus departs. Clumsy in those heavy shoes, she is half-running toward the convent. And incredibly, at such a moment, he catches himself imagining the shifting of pale hips under those clothes, the meaty jiggle, as if that hint of a liaison made by Stefan, fanciful or not, somehow compromised her chastity and justified male lechery, making her fair game for ribaldry and speculation.

Ashamed, he does not call after her, simply watches her flee as if running for her life. Not once does she look back. And he vows that from this moment on, he will stay the hell out of her way, even as he gets it through his head that this creature who has taken him by surprise is no wraith awaiting him under snow-shrouded streetlamps of some cinematic winter city of Old Europe but a live young woman who under kinder circumstances might have accompanied him on the remainder of the journey. At this fateful instant of his life, right before his eyes, this girl whose warmth and lovely form he will never embrace and cherish is vanishing forever as he stands there watching, and he is astonished by the violence of his loss.

FOR TRAVEL TO CRACOW, she is assigned to the first bus, he to the second. Before disappearing through its narrow door, she pauses on the step, gazing about the courtyard, gazing everywhere. Can she be looking for him? Surely she must have discovered by now where he is standing, in the shadow of the portico at the main entrance. Yet she doesn't wave and he won't pressure her by waving or drawing near. Not until the klaxon warns of imminent departure does he give in and lift his hand, good-bye, good-bye. She only turns and disappears inside. No, she cannot have seen him after all; any other explanation is too painful.

Catherine's bus is gone by the time Big Erna shows up in the courtyard. Not that she has come to see anyone off, she boasts, no, no, she just happened by. But to Olin, as he skirts past her on his way to the second bus, she mutters, "It's all taken care of, Baron. He's finished."

"Who's finished? Priest Mikal, you mean?"

"Priest!" She spits that word out viciously and walks away. *Ah Christ*, he thinks. *Shit, shit, shit, shit. There's just no bloody end to it.* "What if he's innocent?" he yells from the doorway as the air brakes wheeze and the bus eases forward. But the big woman does not turn and anyway it's much too late, it's always much too late. *No bloody end to it.*

ALONG THAT STRETCH of road east of Oswiecim, the base of his spine, anticipating, flinches, but Olin refrains from calling attention to the washboard staccato of bus tires where the road traverses the dead railway that vanishes into the forest. In his cramped seat toward the rear, eyes closed, exhausted, he thinks about Catherine and also

Priest Mikal, whose only real offense may be that he is un-prepossessing.

Soon Earwig comes and takes the seat behind him.

"I'm a fucking Romanian," he says. "It's official."

It seems that kind Rainer had heard from Berlin, where wartime archives had been ransacked. About all they had to go on was the very little he could tell them, "but Germans being Germans—" He stops there, frowning. "Don't get me wrong. They went to a lot of trouble. And they found the *Struma*."

The ship *Struma*, an old Danube River scow, had been leased by fleeing Jews for a voyage from Constanta, Romania, over the Black Sea to refuge in Palestine. There the ship was notified that the British quota for Jews entering Palestine was already exceeded; she returned northward as far as Constantinople. Except for a few rich individuals fortunate enough to be "detained" with the captain and first mate at Constantinople, the seven hundred desperate passengers were nowhere permitted ashore. Eventually, engine disabled, stores of food and water exhausted, the derelict ship drifted back and forth on the Bosphorus tides as the Jews swarmed the rails, crying out to passing ships; next, she was dragged north by the Turks into the Black Sea as a hazard to navigation and abandoned some hundred miles off the coast. Here with all passengers she was blown up and sunk by a Russian submarine whose captain was later commended for valor and awarded the suitable medal. (The location of that enemy submarine, not the fate of those aboard, said Rainer, was what had drawn wartime attention in Berlin.) Besides the ten crewmen wearing the ship's life jackets, the lone survivor was a David Stonior, age nineteen, who was picked up by fishermen from the floating wreckage and finally ended up in New York City.

"So you'll go back to New York and try to find him, right?"

"Do I have a choice? Seven hundred screaming Jews. Think he'll remember any names?"

"I don't know," says Olin.

They sit silent for a time. Finally Olin says, "That's a terrible story. Terrible."

"Maybe those Jews had it coming for turning away those good Roma people at Constanta."

"Hey, it's over, man, it's *over*. How do you feel?" And Earwig says, "I don't. *Feel* anything, I mean." He considers Olin. "Which is a lie. How would *you* feel if you'd pissed away your whole damned life for nothing? Who gives a shit—who *ever* gave a shit—about some old Romanian Jew and his useless search? Why did I care so much?" Then he says quietly, "Maybe I just needed to know my name."

SIXTEEN

Earwig will be dropped off at the airport. Before moving up the aisle to take leave of Ben Lama, he mutters a sour sort of thanks to Clements Olin. "You never liked me but you heard me out."

"Matter of fact, I couldn't stand you," Olin says. And because both know that this is true, they can grin ruefully, just once, as they shake hands.

RABBI JIM GLOCK squashes into the aisle seat beside Olin with scarcely a pause in his ongoing plaint. He is grievously disappointed in his death camp experience and "heavy of heart" as well, perceiving all Poland as "one big cemetery." Though the man strikes Olin as doom-ridden and narrow, he has the courage of his own closed mind and a faith strong enough to brandish the Torah's strictures against "that travesty you people call 'the Dancing.'"

The rabbi's skepticism is shared by Anders Stern, who admits he was queerly stirred by the event but has no patience with abstractions as diaphanous as "joy." For most of their companions, however, that nameless joy will not be stifled; it persists on this last afternoon in a debate that grows frenetic in the need to isolate its nature before these firsthand witnesses can scatter, leaving the skeptics to dismiss the strangest experience in all their lives.

The English lady behind Olin is convinced that the joy which arose out of the Dancing was pure ecumenical energy, the pent-up compassion of so many people "bonding" in prayer with others of good will, all striving to bring healing to the martyrs. (Rabbi Glock, glancing Olin's way, rolls his eyes—*Oy vey!*—in the first collegial response these two have shared all week.)

Rainer notes that poor deaf Beethoven was the same notably joyless man who concluded his Ninth Symphony with the triumphal *Ode to Joy*: what, he inquires, was Beethoven's queer "joy" if not transcendence?

Feeling unbearably *alive* in one's own being, as in sexual abandon, Olin reflects—mightn't that draw near it? He recalls how Thoreau had celebrated that vital joy in his atavistic impulse to devour the raw heart of a deer that is slain bare-handed. In similar spirit—this is Ben Lama—the Zen poet Ryokan wrote of a glad willingness to exchange the most magnificent metaphor about the sea for the immediacy, the pure reality, of one splash of cold surf full in the face.

Over and over they inquire about the source of such an unanticipated blessing. Some say it is pure "Love"—like "Truth," Olin reflects, a word half-rotted in most mouths, his own included. Do they mean love of God or love of life or love of the nameless martyrs, the lost millions? Or love right here in this moment for all these disheveled fellow passengers? Love of all hapless humankind, saints, sadists, heroes, perverts, torturers, the lot—in effect, compassion for the human condition, the unconditional acceptance of every last two-legged crotched creature, so isolated and accursed among all beasts in knowing it must die?

Inevitably, their attempts to *understand* grow rarefied, cerebral, words upon dead words. ("All the Universe is one bright pearl," Master Dogen wrote. "What need is there to understand it?") And finally Olin turns away, pressing his forehead to the cold window glass of winter dusk trying to clarify his feelings about Catherine and Mikal and also that confused amateur Jew who sits here with him. *You don't have to be David, remember? But I do.*

As the bus enters the outskirts of the city, he is drawn

back into the debate by something Rabbi Dan is saying about Birkenau. "Without for a moment forgetting the sorrow, there was joy," he says. "People said strange things such as, 'How can I leave?'" Another voice cries, "Yes! That's *it*!" and another, "I felt that same way! Kind of . . . well, you know—*homesick*!" And a Frenchman rarely heard from all that week shocks them all and horrifies himself. "Oh, my beloved Birkenau!" he cries.

"What did he say? Beloved *Birkenau*?" Glock wails. "What kind of sick craziness is *that*?" But the Frenchman in his guilty rapture can only sigh as if entranced, *"Mais oui, c'est ça. C'est Birkenau, mon amour."*

AT THE HOTEL he learns that the first bus was met by a mother superior in a church van. At the front desk, under Olin's name, a page torn from Catherine's diary.

What is this deep presence holding Birkenau together, causing its visitors not to flee in horror but to return down that long road over and over, taking strength from a strange power not fading down with age into the history of long ago but running through the marrow of this earth . . .

"Too romantic, you are thinking, Mr. Clements?" she has written beneath. "Too sentimentable?" Her instinct strikes Olin as rather beautiful. It is also, of course, romantic, "sentimentable."

No signature, no word of parting.

⚜

TO KLEZMER MUSIC at the Ariel restaurant in the old Jewish quarter (where for want of Jews, nosy Anders soon discovers, the management, staff, chefs, and musicians are Christians to a man), they share an oddly festive supper, clinging to the last wisps of exaltation with toasts of the local slivovitz. In candlelight, Olin drinks stolidly as Anders Stern deplores an event in Bosnia the year before, when paramilitary gangs drunk on plum brandy much like this slivovitz had yanked back some seven thousand heads and slit the bared throats of every Muslim boy and man in a detention pen in the town of Srebrenica.

"Der final zolution to der Mushlim Probalem," toasts the Nordic Jew in his thick-spittled rendition of a drunk Serb voice. Struck anew by the ice eyes and shining red lips refracted in Anders's glass, Olin wonders why he had ever found this crude, cruel, yet not unkindly man amusing. (He will recall those eyes another day when he is startled but somehow not surprised by word from Stockholm of the baroque suicide of Dr. Stern.)

DURING SUPPER, the ex-monk Stefan brings word from Oswiecim of an assault on the new priest by local men who dragged him from his altar and rushed him out through the church doors, throwing his vestments after him into the street—a warning, they'd yelled, about what might befall him should he ever dare set foot in town again.

Was Stefan implying that Mikal was—well, that sort of priest? Stefan smiles in his insinuating manner. "One of *those*, you mean?" He shrugs: he only knew that the man had been removed from his parish by the bishop and transferred to Oswiecim—"to lay low, perhaps?"

"*Perhaps?* Isn't this how rumors start?" Olin demands, not offering the man a chair. "In the convent, perhaps? Sister Ann-Marie? Something is missing in your story," says Olin coldly. Where, he wonders, has that poor priest crept tonight?

NEXT MORNING the priest steps out of a doorway just down from the hotel, coat collar turned up against the cold and also to obscure his bruised unshaven face. Tersely he requests money for bus fare, he will pay it back. Fumbling for his billfold, Olin says thinly, "You'll go home, then," by which he means, *Where will you go now, you poor bastard?* The man does not bother to respond. Too violated to thank anyone for anything, he simply waits.

Offered coffee, something to eat, Mikal permits himself to be shown into a café. In a while, sitting up straight and adjusting his ripped collar, he says he has no parish to return to. These days, whole congregations vanish. In Europe, at least, the Church is dying.

"Our disrobed monk says the same thing. You know him?"

"That man never disrobed, not voluntarily," the priest says sharply. "He was defrocked and excommunicated. He is 'dead to us,' as we say in the Church. But I think he has never let go."

It seems that Sister Ann-Marie, upset by an ugly rumor picked up at the convent, must have repeated it to Sister Catherine, which turned Sister Catherine against him. But probably Sister Ann-Marie was not the source.

"You think it was Stefan—"

The other shrugs, uncomfortable. "These days, the mere fact that I was transferred out of my parish might have been enough."

Priest Mikal has tried to forgive Stefan because Stefan himself as an orphaned child raised by the diocese had been molested by a depraved priest. Even so—he knew no other life—Stefan persevered as a seminarian, and later on, as a young brother on the path of holy orders, until he discovered that his molester was still active in another parish and realized that the greater sin would be to remain silent. Denied a hearing, he was browbeaten, bullied, ridiculed, and threatened with eternal damnation until finally he cracked and went along with the coverup. But he had made enemies, and before long his ordination was deferred and he was stripped of his monk's habit. To be refused holy orders was a dreadful blow to a seminarian raised in a church orphanage, a choirboy, an altar boy, who knew no home but the Church. He turned wild and bitter, "obsessed, paranoid, a little crazy, even. Which does not mean he was wrong," adds the priest carefully. But in the end his drunken solicitation of a young postulant novice who had supported his petition would provide the excuse needed by the hierarchy to get rid of him.

"And the girl? The novice?"

"Penance, prayer, probation. Her order has been testing her sincerity by exposing her to the ordeal of the death camp under the guidance of the same priest who had been obliged to report that episode with Stefan." He nods at Olin's astonishment. "Catherine, yes," he says. "It amused the bishop to assign me as her chaplain. Not that my report would make a difference," he added. "No postulant in favor of women in the priesthood could ever be permitted to complete her novitiate, not without public repentance."

"Somehow I don't think she will do that," says Olin, oddly proud of her.

"No," says the priest. "No, I don't believe she will."

Catherine is over-educated for a novice, he tells Olin, and a little willful—a bit deficient in Christian humility, some would say. And when she discovers that advocacy of women's ordination may be reclassified as *delicta graviora*, "a grave sin against the Church," in the same category as the rape of children—

"My God," says Olin. "That's grotesque! Insane!"

"Yes, it is," says the priest. "The Vatican has gone insane."

Olin follows him outside, wishes him luck. Priest Mikal says, "Our calling is becoming impossible for men like me. Though we are a majority in the priesthood, people associate us with those predators, you see, and we are told to stay away from the parish children." He speaks with deep sadness but without malice. "Anyway, I appreciate your concern. Perhaps some agency for refugees abroad can find a use for me."

AT THE MUSEUM, Cecilia Gallerani emerges from the dark of her own alcove upstairs. No one else is present.

Even the custodian has vanished, leaving Olin alone with her in the dead quiet.

Indirect lighting illuminates the pallor of this young Milanese of the Renaissance who holds a tense white winter weasel on her lap. Bought in Italy two centuries ago and presented to her by her son Prince Adam, *Young Woman with Ermine* had been little appreciated and in fact disliked, so he has read, by the museum's founder, Princess Izabela Czartoryski (who, of the ermine, is said to have observed, "If that is a dog, it is a very ugly one"). The princess had its luminous night blue background repainted a funereal black, removing all depth of perspective, and rechristened the portrait *La Belle Ferronnière*, the name already attached to the celebrated Leonardo in the Louvre. Still, the portrait is elegant, the girl pensive and demure in brown wimple and a gray-blue smock worn over her lustrous chestnut robe. The waxy hand that restrains the ermine looks oddly elongated—a consequence, he assumes, of liberties taken with a masterwork by a spoiled princess.

He turns when light footsteps on the stair slow and fall silent.

She stands there in the alcove entrance, gazing past him at Cecilia. She looks somehow not herself.

When he opens his mouth and no sound comes, both take refuge in the painting, as if Count Sforza's child mistress might offer sage advice out of her hard experience of the past. Finally, Catherine says, "So, Clements Olin, you have found her, your young woman with her weasel." And he mutters, froggish, "Do you like her, Catherine?"

"Like?" And still she looks past him, past his gaze. At length she says quietly, "Why I would not like a nice Catholic girl like me?"

With no idea how he should be feeling, far less what he should say, he points out the empty frame still awaiting the missing Raphael. "Never recovered, sadly . . ." But this is just chatter as of course she knows, and she touches his forearm to hush him. "Clements, I, too, I wish to say so much. *Everything!* I feel we are . . . we were . . ."

"Brother and sister in Christ, I believe you said," he reminds her, feeling—what? Weak? Overjoyed? A little cruel? But most of all, afraid—afraid for her, afraid for both of them. His heart pounds as he takes her hands, which she permits without resistance. The hands are inert, so damp and cold that his own hands flinch, faintly repelled.

She senses this: the color leaves her face. In a moment, she looks frightened. Knowing he must give her up right now, once and for all, he tells her stiffly how ashamed he is that he has behaved foolishly; no doubt he has complicated things, caused difficulties. But even his sincerity feels artificial, his smile hideously false. "It's been wonderful to know you. I am truly grateful"—a lame finish fit for the occasion. And only now does he notice why she looks different—that faint blood shading on her lips like the last cool touch of the mortician, that tiny crimson fleck on her front tooth.

Reading his eyes, Catherine knows she has been seen and frees her hands. "So," she murmurs in a strange drowned voice, "I begin again." She moves swiftly to the stairwell, where she pauses with one foot on the first step down. Searching his face as he moves toward her, she is fighting for composure. "You say to me you will come here so I come here, too. To say good-bye. Where you invited me." Her face is pale, her voice a tattered whisper. "So now I say to you, good-bye, Mr. Olin, may God be with you."

"Please, Catherine. Please listen." Listen to what? What can he tell her that makes sense? Nothing comes. Just when he must be resolute, he is struck dumb.

Quick footsteps scatter down the stairwell. The heavy door creaks open and thuds to. He jumps down the stair, bangs through the door. *Wait, wait!* Knowing he must not, he wants to shout her name, run after her, he wants to claim her before all the world, knowing he must not. Her turning up this way means nothing, she'd only come to say good-bye just as she'd said; all he had noticed, after all, was a trace of somebody's old lipstick, no doubt dabbed on for the journey home. For her own sake, he must send her on her way, wasn't that what he'd decided?

She is still moving away.

Her walk is tilted, pulled off-balance by the stiff black

valise that she must have left at the entrance. She's brought her things then! Has she abandoned her novitiate? Been suspended? Or—oh Christ!—has she come on some wild impulse, only to be scared off by his recognition that he'd been a fool?

She is going, soon she will be gone. He does not call. What if he calls and she should stop? Stand there awaiting him? What can he say then?

A cold rain, fitful.

He is running, calling. He overtakes her, reaching for her bag. She will not let go—no protest, simply won't let go, and the strength of her determination awes him. "What's happened, Catherine?" he pleads. "Where are you going?"

She seems not to hear him. In profile, her face looks neither stubborn nor upset. She crosses the great Market Square, blind to the traffic and the rain. Trying to stay abreast, he hurries and stumbles. Panting, he tells her they must stop somewhere and talk a little—that café on this side of the church, okay? "That's the old church Malan told me about, the one with that stained glass—"

But she does not slow as she passes the café, then the church entrance, nor does she look back until he shouts, "Amalia!"

Startled, she pauses. But she does not turn, does not set down the bag, nor does he move forward to take it. He has stopped, too. Yards apart, they stand transfixed for moment after moment. Then something gives way, their time is past, and she sets out again, leaving him torn in half.

Among the precipitous roof peaks, the gray heavens rumble in a distant thunder like cannonades in the grand old Polish wars of long ago. Sheltered from the rain in the church entrance, he watches the blue beret until it disappears around a corner.

THE CHURCH IS EMPTY, the high altar far away. Vaguely, inadvertently, he crosses himself before retreating into a side aisle and taking refuge in a narrow pew. Where a shaft of light warms the faded rose-brown of the narrow cushion, he kneels for a long time in aimless penitence and longing, forehead touched to the dark wood, trying not to think at all, or rather, to feel nothing.

Somewhere on high and out of view, an invisible organist torments the limits of the pipes with loud discordant variations on a Bach chorale. *Wachet Auf, Ruft uns die Stimme*—is that the one? No matter. It cannot distract him from that last sight of her rounding the corner.

Lifting his gaze, he eventually locates Malan's stained-glass window. A thunderous Jehovah brow, a torrent of white beard, cascading downward from on high; the white is soon lost among the livid greens and blues of sun-filled Eden emerging out of chaos. And there it sits, crouched in the swirl of colors—a gray claw with long stiletto nails and carmine veins like lethal wires under the rotting skin, the dead hand of an aghast Almighty withdrawn from His Creation.

In the high windows, ice blues of the firmament pierce wild blood reds; all Heaven has been murdered, set afire. All is impending. The winter sunlight comes and goes, shadows sweep past; the burning panes are lashed by sheets of rain. In that instant, as a sun shaft reignites the colors, the fire blood, the organ shriek, bind his mortal senses hard and tight as a pennant whipped by wind around its pole.

THE LIGHT HAS VANISHED. With time gone dead, he cannot know how long he may have been there. But in a while, as space and time regather, awareness comes that imminence is gone. Of those wild colors, only tints remain; the old church is left in medieval stillness to get on with its decay.

A scary *bang* as the storm doors are thrown wide and wind and rain rush in on gusts of weather. In the surging entranceway, amorphous figures in dark clothing mill and push, pale faces blurred, half-hidden.

There you are again, he thinks. The missing. The near-forgotten.

In the wavering of candles he sits motionless, broken-brained and wholly brokenhearted.

A number of friends deserve full, warm acknowledgment of their kind support throughout the completion of this book, my beloved children and senior Zen students foremost among them. In the pages of such a book, however, a profusion of names and acknowledgments seems intrusive, and so, with regret, most were finally set aside. In a scene of such emptiness and silence, a blank page would be far more to the point.

Even so, a few people must not be left unmentioned. I am grateful as ever to my dear wife, Maria, master chef and gifted closet poet, for her good critical sense and strong, loyal presence; also, my hilarious fishing partner, dry martini virtuoso, and all-around *consigliere,* the writer and editor Stephen Byers, who kept us laughing; and finally, my exceptional assistant, the writer Laurel Berger, whose kind honesty, intelligence, and sharp editorial eye contributed so much to keeping this strange book coherent. The generosity of spirit shown by all three in a hard year has been astonishing.